"How long have you been running the ranch?"

"For a little over a year and a half," Quinn said. Instinct shouted at him to proceed with caution. "Why?"

"Did you give up climbing for this?" Taylor asked.

"Excuse me?"

"I want to know what your priorities are. If you're a rancher, you're a rancher. That's fine. But I didn't hire a rancher to see me through my recertification. I hired you under the express belief you were a dedicated mountaineer."

Muscles along his jaw worked and knotted. "I'm perfectly capable of doing, and being, both."

"I disagree." She crossed her arms and looked at some point well beyond him. "When was the last time you summited, Quinn? Eight months? Twelve? More?" She waved him off when he started to answer. "What you've been doing with yourself over the past several months may not matter so much to you, but it matters very much to *me*."

Dear Reader,

There are times when a book speaks to an author, and this book was one of those times. It was also one of those times when the author spoke back to the book, and not all of the words were amiable. This book challenged me in ways I wasn't prepared to confront, both good and bad. Both the manuscript and the characters pushed me to write with such emotional authenticity that there were days I was literally incapable of making dinner—or even ordering off a menu—because I was so mentally fried! The end result was a book that resonated with me on a unique emotional level and proved worth every ounce of sweat and every minute of sleep lost. May you find yourself as caught up in the tale as I was and, in the end, as enamored with the characters as I am.

Happy reading,

Kelli Ireland

Kelli Ireland

———

Conquering the Cowboy

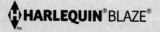
HARLEQUIN® BLAZE®

Recycling programs
for this product may
not exist in your area.

ISBN-13: 978-0-373-79964-0

Conquering the Cowboy

Printed in U.S.A.

Kelli Ireland spent a decade as a name on a door in corporate America. Unexpectedly liberated by fate's sense of humor, she chose to carpe the diem and pursue her passion for writing. A fan of happily-ever-afters, she found she loved being the puppet master for the most unlikely couples. Seeing them through the best and worst of each other while helping them survive the joys and disasters of falling in love? Best. Thing. Ever. Visit Kelli's website at kelliireland.com.

To get the inside scoop on Harlequin Blaze and its talented writers, visit Facebook.com/BlazeAuthors.

All backlist available in ebook format.

Visit the Author Profile page at Harlequin.com for more titles.

To Vivian Arend, a beautiful soul who recognizes the value of a country boy. Muah!

1

WHETHER IT WAS beating the house in Vegas or coming back from a search-and-rescue call that had much higher stakes, Taylor Williams thrived on beating the odds. No, that wasn't quite right. She didn't just *thrive* on it. She *lived* for it, for those moments when she turned the bell curve into a ninety-degree climb and made the competition sweat—not to keep up, but merely keep her within sight, when she forced "average" to recognize her as irrefutably superior.

And if being a member of the Pacific Northwest's Mountain Search and Rescue team, known as the Prime Times, had taught her anything about superiority, it was that staring down long odds—without blinking—was the easy part. Surviving the consequences? That was the ultimate measure of true strength.

Never before had she doubted her ability to survive. Not until the early morning hours of May 17 when the rescuers had become the rescued…and recovered.

She'd lived while her team, and the climber they'd been sent to retrieve, had died.

Sole survivor.

If only she'd been a *soul* survivor.

But she wasn't. Nothing but broken remnants of who she'd been lay scattered around what was left of her life.

Details were scarce. Her memory's recall abilities were less effective than using six feet of rope for a twelve-foot descent—she'd get halfway there and hang. The entire event had narrowed down to a few mental snapshots and a handful of sensory memories—a sound, a word, a smell. Nothing more. Her only recourse had been to read the After Action Review, and she had. Exhaustively. She'd tried to fill in the blanks, tried to piece together what had gone so wrong, until she now possessed every detail known to the crash-site investigators. Those facts were efficient. Factual. Cold. Few.

Page one: Team Leader Taylor Williams requested helo OH-58 Bell Jet Ranger in response to a distress call received at 17:52 from a lone climber who identified himself as Gary Wilcox, age 29.

He'd had blue, blue eyes.

Had.

Past tense.

Her fist balled against her thigh.

She pounded the steering wheel of her Toyota Tundra. A sharp beep sounded, and she jerked the wheel. Deep substrate along the side of the road sucked the passenger tires down. Gravel flew as the truck fishtailed. Her control slipped.

"No!" A short scream was ripped from her throat as her gaze shot to the instrument panel. No. The dash. Not the instrument panel.

Truck. Not a helo. I'm on the ground.

Her fuel light flickered once…twice…before glowing bright orange against the dark dashboard.

Regaining control of the truck, she slowed and, finally, stopped. All around her, the Sangre de Cristo Mountains rose, rock faces reflecting the afternoon sun even as, well above the tree line, a spattering of snow dotted the highest peaks. Wrapping her arms around her middle, she leaned forward and rested her forehead against the steering wheel.

Not Rainier. Nothing like Rainier.

Memories that always hovered just out of conscious reach left her wondering, for what seemed like the millionth time, if she might have changed the ultimate outcome, might have saved lives versus costing them, had she made different choices, been five minutes earlier or ten seconds later to the scene. Perhaps if she had, she wouldn't have been required to spend the last several months in intensive therapies, physical and psychological, trying to come to grips with her injuries and worse— much, much worse—the loss of her team.

Survivor's guilt swelled into monster emotional waves not even the best psychiatrists had been able to teach her to surf. Those waves peaked and then crashed, the impact rolling through her like a detonation. Her chest seized and air became a commodity so scarce she didn't have an emotional credit with a deep enough credit line to get what she needed. Fighting off the looming panic attack, Taylor forced her hands to relax, but not before her blunt fingernails had left deep crescent marks in the flesh of her palms. The panic, and her response, had become so predictable. She hated that and fought to push the panic away. To control her breathing. To ban the memories she couldn't completely access. To block the total recall she had where the factual reports were concerned.

Her last therapist called this type of reaction "extreme avoidance." Taylor preferred to call it "critical self-preservation," because if she didn't? If she couldn't find the strength to fight back? She was done. The bottom line didn't change, though. Her reaction could be interpreted a hundred different ways, but the ultimate explanation was the simplest, the most consistent. Her head was a freaking mess. But Taylor was going to change that. Fate, Karma and all their cousins could kiss her ass.

A semi blew past her, rocking her four-wheel-drive truck on its shocks. The vehicle settled long before she'd convinced herself to lift her forehead and take in the fuel gauge's digital display, which read 48 Miles. She'd better find fuel, and fast. The last town lay much farther behind her than that. Hell, it had been nearly half an hour since she'd seen another car.

A quick tap on the GPS and the electronic voice, male with a slight British accent—she'd named him Daniel early on the first day of this unsanctioned trip—advised she was only eleven miles from her destination.

Crooked Water, New Mexico.

A late-model pickup passed her, then brake lights glowed as the truck slowed.

Crap. She did *not* need help. Fumbling with her blinker, she checked her mirror, found empty highway in both directions and pulled back onto the asphalt. She didn't look at the driver of the truck but instead gave an absent wave as she passed him. A sigh of relief escaped when she glanced in her rearview mirror and saw him make his way back onto the road. Confrontation avoided. As small a town as Crooked Water was reputed to be, she knew people would be curious, knew there would be questions. That's why she'd booked herself into the tiny rental at the Rocking-B Ranch. The place had no reviews and seemed to have been listed on the online rental site only in the last couple of weeks. She'd simply tell anyone who asked that she was a guest there. While it was true, the answer served a bigger purpose. It meant she didn't have to tell them the real reason she'd come to New Mexico.

"Your destination is ahead."

"Thanks, Daniel," she said, reaching out to mock fist-bump the GPS.

The word *unsanctioned* tripped through her mind, rolling around as she crested a hill and the first signs of civilization appeared. This personal expedition certainly hadn't been approved by anyone—her boss, her doctor, her physical therapist or her psychiatrist. But she needed to start taking some of her own back. Getting here was the equivalent of learning to crawl. Braving the fears she'd face as she prepped for the climb would equate to the first time she'd stood on her own two feet. And the four-day recertification climb she'd booked?

Her palms went cold and sweaty, her heart rate ratcheting up to jackhammer level in seconds.

It was the climb that was all about her learning to walk again. Neither her mind nor her body's systems cared that the "walking" she'd be doing was figurative. All she could think about was falling.

Literally.

Her hand fisted so tight her knuckles bleached out to a skeletal white. "Not going there."

Pulling off at the first gas station she saw, she set the pump to fill her tank and crossed the lot to use the tiny, unisex restroom. Splashing water on her pasty face didn't do anything but make her look pale *and* wet.

"Excellent. I'm proof the walking dead *can* tolerate daylight," she muttered, pulling her ball cap off and finger combing her hair. She pulled the mass back and tucked it up in a sloppy topknot. Best she could do at the moment. Another final glance at the mirror revealed hazel eyes, too wide, dark brows parked under a seemingly perma-creased forehead and a mouth that had forgotten how to smile. The V-neck of her T-shirt offered some decent cleavage, though. An unladylike sound—half hiccup, half snort—escaped. She was comedy and tragedy all rolled into one, but comedy didn't have its game face on.

Crossing the lot to her truck, she hung up the pump nozzle, took her receipt and boosted herself into the cab again. Only habit, and certainly not the nonexistent traffic, had her looking both ways before she pulled back onto Highway 39 and continued west. It took more energy than she typically had this time of day to force herself to pay attention to the winding road. The Sangre de Cristo Mountain Range rose around her in stunning glory, the peaks of each granite precipice defying the tree line and piercing an impossibly blue sky. Late spring and the temperatures were still cool, but the forecast said the weather would hold for the climb.

Sweat created instant half-moons on the fabric under her armpits, the moisture stolen straight from her mouth.

Her stomach dove for the soles of her feet, and she swallowed back the seemingly ever-present bile that kept her throat raw.

I'm probably going up one of those peaks.

No, not probably. The climb was happening. No backing out.

"Not alone," she whispered to herself. "I'm not going to be alone."

She'd have Quinn Monroe, owner of Legendary Adventures, as her climbing partner.

He was notorious in the mountaineering community. Considered one of the best in North America, he'd climbed all over the world. He'd be a strong enough partner and professional instructor to help her shed this unrelenting fear and regain her confidence. Unless she managed the class with success, there was no way she'd be able to complete her recertification as an alpine guide and wilderness first responder nurse for the National Park Service.

She might have neglected to mention her, well, neuroses in her email correspondence with Mr. Monroe, but he'd find out soon enough. Hiring the best of the best had been her only hope of getting through this, so they'd both deal with the repercussions of her omission when it became necessary. Until then? It wasn't relevant.

Her initial obstacle would be getting through the refresher course. She'd have to hold it together long enough to make the trek to the base of the climb. Then she'd gear up and the truth would be out there. She had to recertify if she wanted to keep her job as the team leader for the National Park Service's Search and Rescue Team, or SRT. Recertification was standard for any team member who had been involved in a rescue attempt that had resulted in the death of a team member, but as a team lead who'd lost all five members of her team and the climber they'd gone after?

She readjusted her sunglasses and tried to swallow the lump of truth lodged in her throat.

If she failed, there were no second chances. She'd be out of a job, without a certification. She could go into clinical nursing, but a hospital setting didn't suit her. She'd be miserable. *Beyond* miserable.

Since the accident, her employer had been compassionate as well as generous, holding her job while granting her more than the mandatory recovery period. But compassion only carried an employee for so long. Management had begun making noises about her getting back to work, prompting her boss, Greg, to call.

"Your name's been coming up at management's roundtable meetings. HR is all over me to get a firm return-to-work date from you."

Tension had formed an invisible noose that tightened around her throat. "I told you I'm working on it."

"They're asking for something in writing."

"What, my word's no good?" she demanded, nausea forming a greasy film that coated her stomach lining.

"You *are* coming back, right?"

"That's always been the plan."

"Then give them something, Taylor." Greg's voice had been solid but somber. "Tell them you'll get your re-cert by whatever day and you'll be back a week after that." He'd paused. "Whatever date you pick, keep in mind that sooner would be better."

The unspoken truth had been there, suspended on the airwaves between her cell and his. She would either get herself together and get back to work or management would cut her loose.

So she'd make that first, and only, attempt to face the mountain and complete her recertification climb...or she wouldn't. If she couldn't do it, if she couldn't conquer this fear of heights or, more specifically, of *falling* from significant heights, she'd be done. Out of work.

And probably over the edge.

DUST OBSCURED EVERYTHING in the rearview mirror as Quinn Monroe pulled onto the highway. The shoulder medium—fancy way to say *dirt*—was so dry his tires fought for purchase. The county needed rain. Bad. The harsh conditions were what had prompted him to stop and offer to help the owner of the out-of-state tag that had pulled onto the shoulder, the driver resting his head on the steering wheel. This was no place for vacationers to get lost, run out of gas or need a bottle of chilled spring water. Big-city conveniences didn't exist out here. Hell, *nothing* existed out here but grassland, cows, mountains and the handful of human souls who called Crooked Water, New Mexico, home.

Home.

If someone had suggested to Quinn even five years ago that he'd be back in the remote little village for more than just a visit, that he'd come back to this godforsaken place for good, he would have called the guy a liar. Sure, he may have grown up here, but he'd never been at home, never felt like part of the community or part of something bigger than himself. That's what he'd been looking for when he left more than a decade ago. And damn if he hadn't found it—only to lose it and wind up back here, after all.

His focus shifted, drifting away from the road, across the grassland and up the foothills before settling on the peaks of the Sangre de Cristo Mountains. *That* was where he belonged—in the mountains, on the mountain face, granite under his fingertips. Not here.

I was never meant for this life.

Sunshine glinted on metal in the field south of the highway and Quinn glanced that way instinctively. Muscles in his stomach tightened at the sight of the windmill, the tail wagging back and forth to keep the lazily spinning fan faced into the wind.

Forcing himself to refocus on the two-lane highway, he tried to keep his mind on the faded yellow and white lines in front of him.

No dice.

It had been almost eighteen months since the middle-of-the-night phone call that had changed everything. Eighteen months back here, home, in New Mexico. His heart ached with loss and longing.

Rolling onto one hip without slowing, he pulled his smartphone out of the back pocket of his Wranglers. A single press of the home key showed no missed calls. He'd become paranoid about being inaccessible, and cell service out here was sporadic at best, nonexistent at worst.

Five bars of service.

No missed calls.

The ringer was on.

Volume was up.

A small part of him relaxed. The rest of him remained as knotted up as ever.

Memories crowded in on him, despite his objections, and for a split second Quinn wasn't in his truck headed to town. He was in bed in his little Idaho home, the alarm set unreasonably early so he'd be on time for a scheduled climb up Baron Spire. The ringer on his smartphone had been shut off, the vibrate function left on in case his parents needed him. And they had.

Mom.

She'd called four times in a row, the phone eventually shimmying its way across the nightstand and over the edge, hitting the floor with a *thunk* that pulled him out of deep, dreamless sleep. He'd rolled over, blindly fishing around on the floor for the phone, accidentally hitting Answer before he had the phone to his ear.

Soft sobs came from the caller.

Adrenaline had careened through his system and driven his heart wild, setting his nerves on edge and sharpening his voice. "Mom?"

No answer.

"Mom?" he'd asked again, undiluted fear souring his stomach. He had fallen out of bed then, his knees striking the hardwood floor with a loud *crack*. He'd buried his face in his hands and the phone had slipped, forcing him to re-pin it between his ear and shoulder to hear her.

Odd thing to remember.

"You need to come home, Quinn."

"Where's Dad?" he'd demanded. "Put Dad on the phone, Mom." Pleaded. "Where is he?" Beseeched.

"This afternoon…" She'd hiccuped, a sharp sound. "Oh, Quinn…" Deep breaths had raked across the phone's receiver, scraping at him through the earpiece.

"Tell me."

Then she'd done as he'd asked. He'd stopped breathing the moment she complied, uttering damning words he wanted to childishly demand she take back. "Your dad was working on the windmill in the south pasture. No one is sure what happened. Not exactly. All we know is that he fell. The doctor said his injuries were massive. Quinn, he didn't…"

The words "make it" weren't spoken, but they were there just the same as if they had been shouted, hovering a moment before they crashed into him. The impact tattooed the truth on his heart. And then? The world simply stopped.

His dad. The man Quinn had spent years following, listening to, emulating. The man who had convinced Quinn it was okay to want more than the rural lifestyle he'd grown up with. The man who'd handed him the title to his pickup and $15,000 in cash, telling Quinn to figure out what made him happy and where he'd be happiest doing it. The man who'd been unashamedly in love with his wife and left a light on for his only child every night.

His heart had seized, a tight band of pain around his chest. He couldn't breathe. Couldn't think.

Dad.

A jackrabbit darted across the road and he jerked the wheel. "Pay attention," he muttered to himself.

More than eighteen months since he'd lost the man and Quinn still felt off-center, like the world had tilted hard to the left and he couldn't get it back on its axis.

When he crested the small hill, the town appeared as if conjured by dark memories that defied the impossibly blue sky. It looked exactly as it had when he'd left twelve years ago. He chuffed out a harsh laugh as he realized that there was as little for a man of thirty-one to do here as there was a nineteen-year-old boy on the edge. Nothing had changed. Not a single. Damn. Thing.

"Except that one half of the best part of this place is gone." His words were swallowed by the noise his all-terrain tires made on the rough asphalt road.

Stomach rumbling, he shot a look at the clock. It was late for lunch. He could skip it altogether, head to the ranch and snag something from his mom's fridge or—he turned onto Main Street—he could grab a bite in town. The cook at Muddy Waters, the local bar and grill, was an old high school buddy. He'd throw a burger on the grill without complaint and Quinn would be sure to tip the waitress well. His stomach growled in response. A burger it was.

He parked curbside, hopped down from his truck and traversed the fractured concrete walk that never failed to trip up drunks and tourists alike.

Inside, the atmosphere was comfortable in its familiarity. Square laminate tables, each surrounded by four vinyl-covered chairs, were scattered around the floor.

He nodded to a handful of familiar faces as he settled at a table in the corner and dropped his hat on the neighboring chair.

The waitress sauntered up, order pad and pen in hand. "What'll it be, handsome?"

He didn't even bother with the menu. "Cheeseburger, medium, all the trimmings, large basket of onion rings and a lemonade. How's your mom, Amy?"

The waitress was another high school friend, and her family had owned the restaurant for three generations.

She rolled her eyes. "Same as always. Swears I'm running this place into the ground and am going to end up being forced to sell to an—" she feigned a gasp "—*outsider*. She's threatening to come out of retirement."

Quinn chuckled. "If she comes back, tell her she'll have to make her chocolate cream pies by the dozen. I miss those."

"Secret family recipe I just happen to possess." She considered him for a moment before tacking on, "You should come to dinner one night. I'll make you a pie."

He appreciated her predicament, being single in Crooked Water. The dating pool was more mud puddle than pond. But as much as Quinn liked her, he wasn't the solution to her problem.

He'd once thought he wanted a love like his parents had shared, had spent years looking for it, dating, hoping every new face was The One. It hadn't taken him long to realize exactly how rare that kind of love was. And now, given what he'd seen his dad's death do to his mom? He intended to avoid relationships at all costs. No amount of love could make that amount of grief worth it.

Looking up at Amy, he smiled. "I appreciate the offer, but I have to pass. With Dad gone, Mom needs all the help she can get. Keeps my priorities at home, making sure she's taken care of."

The waitress smiled. "Can't blame a girl for asking."

"I'm flattered you did."

She tucked her pen into her topknot of hair and ripped his order off the pad. "I'll turn this in. Hank should have it out in just a few."

He settled back to wait, sliding down in his chair to stretch his legs out in front of him.

"I hear you're taking someone up the mountain," Art Jameson, a town local and family friend, called out across the vacant dance floor. "That mean you're back to climbing again, Q?"

Every eye in the place landed on Quinn.

He had no idea how the news had reached the gossip mill, but it clearly had. And he wasn't ready to answer. Mostly because he didn't have a damn clue what to say.

There'd been speculation that he'd be out of Crooked Water and back on the ropes before the seasons changed. But he hadn't. Not this season, anyway. He was still grieving his dad's passing, for Pete's sake. More than that, his mom needed him. None of that mattered. People around here were fascinated that he'd left home and made something of himself. And since Jeff, the guy who'd bought Quinn's former business, had referred this climber to Quinn—the first client of his *new* climbing business—he had expected folks would discover he was going up the mountain again. Next, word would get out he was opening up shop as a full-time guide. Managing that news would be…difficult, at best, seeing as he hadn't discussed it with his new ranching partner.

His mom.

Fighting the urge to pull his shoulders up around his ears and growl, he instead met Art's curious gaze with his level one. "I never really quit."

Sam Tolbert, the region's large animal veterinarian, picked up his tea glass and tipped it in Quinn's direction. "Heard you agreed to take some climber up Trono del Cielo next week."

Trono del Cielo. The Throne of Heaven.

Quinn arched a brow as he slid lower in the hardbacked diner chair. "Gone a handful of years and the only thing to have changed around here is the gossip mill's efficiency."

This, *this*, was what he hated about small towns. You

couldn't switch toilet paper brands without someone noticing and "mentioning" it to someone else.

"Rumors come and go, Doc. Hang around long enough and time will let you know what's true." Grabbing his hat, he stood, slapped it on his head and searched Amy out in the small crowd. "Make that a to-go order, would you?" He needed to get out of here. The levee of polite restraint had been publicly breached. People would ask what they wanted to know, pose question after question that he didn't want to answer. He wasn't prepared for that and was pretty sure he wouldn't live to see the day he was.

"Hank was just plating it. I'll wrap it, instead."

"Thanks." Quinn tipped his chin, first toward Art and then Doc as he passed their table. "You boys mind yourselves. And don't you go flirting too much with Miss Amy here without your wife's express consent, Art."

The older men chuckled, and Art nodded at the young woman. "Too much respect for Miss Amy to put her through the missus's jealous rage."

Amy snorted. "Betty would probably send *me* spousal support if I'd take your sorry ass off her hands."

Everyone in the bar laughed, louder this time, and Quinn relaxed as he felt the interest in him shift away. "What do I owe you?"

"Nine and a quarter," Amy said, smile wide. "Plus the tip you would've left, of course."

"Wouldn't have it any other way." Quinn handed her several bills and took the sack of food she offered him. "Thanks for this."

"Sure. You want your drink to go?"

"Nah. I'll pop over to the mercantile and grab something. I have a list of things to pick up before I head home, anyway. Thanks, though."

He turned for the door, and a question he hadn't been prepared for hit him in the back.

"You coming to the barn dance at the Hendersons' place Friday night?" Doc Tolbert asked. "Bring Elaine if you do. She'd probably enjoy a night out."

Everyone paused and waited for him to answer.

Quinn shot the vet a quick, steady look. "You want Mom to go, you ask her directly. Not me."

Several people chuckled, but the humor was strained.

"I'm asking you as a matter of courtesy," the vet responded, level and calm.

"She's a grown woman who knows her own mind." The words sounded tinny in his head, sort of far away. Denial at its best. No *way* was Sam asking after Elaine as anything but friends. Sure, his mom was a widow, but that didn't make her single. As in datable. Not now, and maybe not ever.

Definitely not in Quinn's eyes.

2

TAYLOR SANG ALONG with the radio and Toby Keith as he professed why he should've been a cowboy. Pulling into town, Taylor reached up and turned the radio off. Nothing in the online ad for the little cabin she'd booked had prepared her for the reality of arriving in Crooked Water, New Mexico.

Not even close.

Slowing to the posted speed limit of thirty-five miles per hour, she had plenty of time to assess the town. All of it. The sign outside the tiny village advertised a population number someone had taped over with duct tape and, using stencils and spray paint, modified to 207. There was a post office housed in a glass-faced stucco building that couldn't be more than twenty-five feet square.

Beside it sat a brick-bodied bar and grill with a neon sign over the front door that buzzed loud enough she could hear it.

Directly across the street was a mercantile-cum-grocer with touristy knickknacks set in the plate glass window. Sale ads were hand drawn with permanent marker on fluorescent paper and peppered the remaining window space.

And a block farther down, set apart from what seemed

to be the heart of the town, a small white chapel faced off
with a windowless drive-thru liquor store.

Parking in front of the Muddy Waters Bar and Grill, she
hopped down from her truck and strolled across the street.
Somewhere nearby, Quinn Monroe waited. She wasn't
slated to meet him until the day after tomorrow, but she'd
wanted some time to settle into her little cabin at the ranch.

That's a load of crap and you know it, her subconscious
snarked. *You wanted to scope the climb and afford yourself
plenty of time to skulk out of town if it looked too tough.
At least have the good grace to wait for the bartender to
hand you that first double shot of whiskey before you start
lying to yourself.*

Man, if her inner voice grew any more compassionate, she'd have to think about finding a way to suffocate
the witch.

She pushed through one of the large doors to the mercantile and stopped, door still half open. Generic canned
chili—a *lot* of generic canned chili—had been built into
a pyramid display right inside the entry. A large sign pro-
claimed "BOGO! Get it before it's gone!"

"How much chili can a community of barely two hundred people *eat*?" she asked quietly, still frozen halfway
through the doorway.

"Oh, you'd be surprised," a tiny, bespectacled man answered from a stool behind an ancient register.

He was so diminutive in a wizened way that it took her
a second to realize he'd stood. Shuffling around the end
of the worn pine counter with its aluminum flashing and
green glass candy jars, he couldn't have topped out at more
than five foot three inches.

"Get fishermen in here all damn day who think they'll
pull a Bear Grylls and live off the land. Bunch of morons,
the lot of 'em. More men end up with food poisoning from

trying to cook their catch over an open fire and forage for greens along the riverbanks than those eatin' at my sister's diner over in Boise." He gazed up at her with rheumatic, watery blue eyes and grinned. "Works out for me, though. Buy-one-get-one-free chili is mighty tasty when you've had the dysentery in the wilds. Got a special on Charmin, too, for that matter, but you don't look like a moron."

Lips quivering, Taylor stepped the rest of the way in and let the door fall shut before she burst out laughing. It had been so long since she'd let loose, her facial muscles ached with it. Bent over, hands on her knees, she glanced up to find the old man grinning even wider. "And the locals?" she couldn't help but ask.

"We don't touch that canned, preservative-filled crap. Anything with a shelf life of eight years is bound to kill you," he said, gesturing across the street with a small jerk of his chin. "Town folk eat at Muddy Waters."

"What's good over there?" she asked absently as she peered down the store's aisles. The place was admittedly well stocked for such a small, remote grocery.

The little man shrugged. "Just about everything." Then he held out a hand twisted by years of arthritis and roughed by physical work. "I'm Joseph Cummings. You can call me Joe. And if you're here long enough, Old Joe."

She shook his hand, surprised at the strength in his grip. "Hey, Joe. I'm Taylor Williams. I'll be here a little over a week. I'm climbing Trono del Cielo." She swallowed hard at the last bit, not at all sure why she'd offered a stranger the information.

He cocked his head to one side, considering her. "You're the one going up the mountain with Quinn Monroe, then."

"I am, yes. Why?"

"He mentioned he had someone booked for the climb when he came in and ordered provisions." He waved a hand dismissively, shuffling around the counter to reclaim his seat as he spoke. "Couldn't be no one better to lock yourself onto for that climb."

The idea of being locked together, of carabiners tying her fate, her very *survival*, to another's—and his to her—made her swallow convulsively. Gear could fail. Decisions made under pressure, decisions not carefully weighed and measured, could be wrong. Do-overs weren't a given but a matter of grace, and if life lacked one thing, it was grace.

"Good to know," she croaked out.

He carried on, not seeming to notice the sweat suddenly trickling down her temples. "Got a small storefront here, but we do a bang-up catalog order business. I might be older than a petrified dinosaur turd, but I'm good with a computer." His fragile-looking chest puffed up. "I can get you anything I need from my Santa Fe supplier or with my laptop, so you need something while you're here, something I ain't got on the shelf? Just let me know."

"I'll do just that. Thanks."

Joe's eyes narrowed. "You nervous about the climb or meeting Quinn?"

So he had *noticed.* "Why would I be nervous about meeting Quinn?" she asked, avoiding the first part of the question.

The old man cackled. "You're a woman, ain't ya?"

"Yeah, but my breasts don't tend to get too intimidated by the male species." She grinned. "They have a bit of a narcissistic side."

"Rightly so," he said, winking and, of all things, causing her to blush as the door swung open behind her, a rush of hot, dry air washing over the sweat at the nape of her neck. "But Quinn? Well, he's famous in these parts for lovin' and leavin' in nothing flat. Broke a lot of hearts when he left town that first time. Imagine it'll be the same when he leaves this time."

"Good thing I'm just here for the climb, then, isn't it, Joe? That'll keep us both safe."

"Safe?"

"No chance of falling for someone if you go into things knowing he's a one-trick pony prick."

"Not too far off the mark but for one thing," said a deep, smooth voice from behind her. "My bag of tricks is bottomless."

The depth of the newcomer's voice rooted her in place. Taylor couldn't have moved if the hem of her jeans caught fire. She couldn't turn. Couldn't face the man at her back.

Joe laughed, the sound part wheeze, part cough. "Quinn, this here's Taylor Williams."

"Nice to meet you, *Ms.* Williams," he said, voice cool and detached.

Oh, man. "Somehow I doubt that's true, Mr. Monroe."

"Is it safe to assume you're the climber I've been exchanging emails with? The one who recently hired me to obtain his recertification?" His voice, the pitch deep but smooth, sent a shiver up her spine.

"*Her* recertification, and yes. That's me. I'm her."

"You didn't tell me you're a woman," he said, the accusation clear.

"It shouldn't matter, seeing as my gender has nothing to do with my ability to get up or down a mountain, Mr. Monroe."

"Since you've discussed my prick and its tricks with our local grocer, you've invoked the discussion on gender. It also seems more personal if you go ahead and call me Quinn."

Taylor closed her eyes and buried her face in her hands. Only one thought ran through her head. The burning heat of abject humiliation would keep her warm when the desert nights grew cold.

QUINN MONROE HADN'T expected Taylor Williams to show up early. He also hadn't expected Taylor to be, well, a *woman*. But from the slim column of her neck to the end of long, seriously toned legs and the very fine ass parked right between the two, Taylor looked like she was *all* woman. That Old Joe had been giving her the standard spiel about Quinn's reputation was further proof. The grocer must've taken to her quickly. Otherwise he never would've felt the need to warn her to mind herself around him. Unless Joe was just screwing around. You never could tell with him.

Curiosity ate at Quinn and he wondered if her face was as expressive as the unblemished skin of her neck. The red flush that had raced across that pale expanse had been telling. It struck him then that she was incredibly pale for such a highly accomplished climber. Clearly she'd been out of the sun long enough to lose the tan every climber sported. But why? Only way to get the answers he wanted was to ask. Crossing his arms over his chest, he let a smile play around his lips and unquestionable desire burn in his gaze. "If you're going to disparage my capabilities, Ms. Williams, at least face me when you do." When she hesitated, he said softly, "Turn around."

She turned her head just enough to keep him from seeing her face when she answered. "We're not on the mountain yet, *Mr. Monroe*. You don't dictate what I do and don't do until I'm geared up and paying you for your expertise."

Sassy and able to shrug off his surliness. He liked the combination. She'd need it once they hit the mountain, where he would call every shot. Further intrigued, he found himself closing the distance between them and pushing her a little harder. "According to Old Joe, my reputation is that I have specific expertise you don't have to pay for." *High school reputations died hard in a small town...if they died at all.* "To get it, you'll have to turn around."

Ah, that got her going.

Spinning, she faced him, her hazel eyes bright with fury and her mouth working silently.

Then, in a voice so deep and sultry he felt it wrap around him like a silken noose, she lit into him. "Excuse me, Mr. Monroe, but did you just *proposition* me? I'm your client, not some…some…two-bit, cheap-thrill, 'experience-seeking'—" she emphasized it with air quotes "—tour-on out here looking to 'climb your mountain' and stroke your ego every step of the way as you critique my physical form instead of critiquing my climb approach. Clear?"

Joe laughed so hard Quinn couldn't help but worry the old man would choke on his dentures.

Whatever.

Quinn consumed Taylor in one visual gulp. She was roughly six inches shorter than his six foot three, fine boned and lean with defined muscle, but she owned her body and her space like she was his size. Tendrils of hair escaped the edge of her ball cap to trail down her neck and over her shoulders, and he had the most ridiculous urge to see her without the hat. He wanted to set that mass of wavy hair free, wanted to know how long it was, wanted to see it frame her face.

An erotic image of it playing across her bare breasts caught him off guard and he shook his head. He didn't react to women. They reacted to him. It had been the natural order of things since eleventh grade, when twelfth-grader Marcy Jacobs had hauled him into the tack room in her parents' barn and taught him things about older women. Not since then had he allowed a woman to cause every rational thought to vacate his brain, and he wasn't going to start now. He just had to figure out how to retrieve the logical thoughts that had already fled without his consent. In the meantime, he looked her over with what was, at best, open interest and, at worst, carnal intent.

What happened next shocked him and left him scrambling to get his brain back in gear, if for no other reason than to save his pride.

She stepped into his space and glared up at him, going toe-to-toe without batting an eye. "I *know* you did *not* just tell me to turn around so you could…could…take my physical measure and decide whether or not you deem me worthy of your bag of tricks." When he didn't answer, because he *couldn't*, she shoved him hard enough he was forced to step aside as she stormed past him on her way to the door. "You'll have to excuse me, Mr. Monroe. The collision of your reputation with your self-adoration has created a testosterone-dense fallout that's making me nauseous. I need some fresh air."

He watched her long-legged strides eat up the pavement as she crossed the street. She yanked open the door to a familiar truck—the same one he'd stopped to help on the highway—and all but launched herself inside, slamming the driver-side door closed behind her. Reverse lights flared, she backed out of her parking spot and, with a chirp of tires, took off down Highway 39.

"You just made a colossal mistake, boy," Joe hooted.

Quinn glanced over at Old Joe and went with the one thing he knew to be true. "Yeah? Well, she's my client." The first client he'd had since he'd gone live with his new adventure guide business and website. He needed this climb to go well. Months spent racking his brain had yielded little in terms of ways to help his mom make ends meet. The only thing that made any sense at all was to put his skills to use locally. He more than wanted this venture to work. He *needed* it to. Quinn had to find a way to bring in the extra income his dad had earned cowboying for others in order to cover the lean years on their own small place, and no one was hiring Harding County's version of the prodigal son.

"She's a woman who deserves respect, is what she is." Joe looked up with a kind of seriousness that wasn't at all common on that old face. "I know you and your mama have been through hell. Especially your mama. I can't imagine losing my wife, Josie, after more than sixty years married." He shook his head, light glinting off his pate. "But if gossip's right and you intend to stick around and help your mama keep the family ranch running, you're going to have to set aside your pride, and not just this once, mind you. There's no room for pride when you're clawing your way up from hell's own belly."

Quinn stared at his boots, considering.

"Hurts to have your pride lashed by an old man's tongue, I know. My old man was brilliant but brutal with it, so I've been there and more than once." Old Joe leaned on the counter. "Go on after her and tell her you're sorry. It'll likely hurt your pride, but no man's pride has ever caused him to bleed out. Besides, it's your best shot of making something of this climbing thing."

Quinn's eyes nearly bugged out of his head. "Make something?"

Joe waved him off. "I know all about your accomplishments and records and such. Stuff you've done in the *past*," he said, dragging out the last word. "I don't give a rat's patooty about what *was*. Can't change it anyhow. I care about what *is* and what *might be*. I don't want to see your mama hurt again because her son followed in the father's footsteps and put pride out front just waitin' for the fall. Say you're sorry to the lady. It won't kill you, boy."

Quinn considered Old Joe, then gave him a quick nod. "You have that order ready that Mom called in?"

"Been boxed up and waiting on you since yesterday."

Quinn settled the tab and thumbed through the dollar bills in his wallet. All four of them. Heading to his truck with two boxes of necessities, he mentally rerouted his trip home. He'd stop by the bank and see what it would take to get an extension on the ranch's credit line. While he was there, he'd withdraw a little cash to keep on hand for incidentals and cash-only emergencies.

He chuffed out a strained laugh. If things kept on like they had been, the money would be gone before the week's end. It seemed everything had been an emergency of late, from the tractor breaking down and requiring special-order parts to the unanticipated replacement of the septic tank down at the bunkhouse.

The money he'd made selling his mountaineering business before coming back to Crooked Water had been good, and he'd really believed it would cover enough of the bills and buy him enough time to see his mom settled and secure. Then he had planned on figuring out where he'd go and what he'd do when he got there.

But the costs of keeping the ranch afloat had been staggering, and he'd watched the money flow from his account faster than water disappeared down a storm drain during monsoon season. With less than $10,000 left, he'd been forced to find a way to change the flow from solely *out* to at least something coming *in*.

He'd tried odd jobs, day jobs and more, but nothing ever panned out. With no options left, he'd quietly set up a website and begun reaching out to old contacts and looking for one-time climbs and such. Taylor had come to him through one of those channels. He'd initially hesitated. A re-cert would mean a solid week, maybe a little more. But the money… A short-notice, one-on-one recertification course demanded a hefty premium. In the end, the cash was too much of an incentive to turn down, his need for it too great.

He'd signed the contract.

And now here he was, getting ready to find his student and apologize for behaving like an ass. Because he had, and he knew it. That didn't make the apology any easier.

Thoughts running amok, he stopped beside the bed of his truck and deposited the boxes near the cab before opening the driver's door. A wall of heat hit him, the air infused with the leftovers of his burger and onion rings. The smell was so heavy and dense he nearly choked. Finishing lunch was clearly off the day's agenda. Grabbing the grease-stained brown paper bag with the diner's logo printed on the side, he tossed it into the bed of his truck and then climbed into the cab. First priority, windows down and heat wave be damned. That smell had to go.

And second...

Taking a deep breath and shaking his head in disbelief at what he was about to do, he cranked the truck's engine, looked down the street in the direction Taylor had gone and backed out of his parking slot.

Quinn had an apology to deliver.

3

IRRITATION CHASED TAYLOR down State Road 120, pushing the speedometer well to the right of the posted speed limit. She muttered to herself, saying aloud everything she wished she'd thought to say to Quinn Monroe when she'd faced off with him. Smart, cutting remarks that would have made an impression. But no. Not Taylor. The most she'd been able to do was call him a "one-trick pony prick" and storm off.

"Way to go, Williams," she groused, yanking her hat off and tossing it onto the empty passenger seat. A tug on her hair tie was punctuated by a curse, and both were followed up by a hard yank, but her hair came down. She finger combed the mess of waves, but nothing less than a hot shower and a quart of conditioner would tame the flyaway thing she had going on. She'd get settled in her little cabin, eat whatever the owner sent over for supper, since she hadn't picked up anything at the mercantile, and then she'd get a good night's sleep. Tomorrow had to be better. Right?

Her opinionated subconscious remained silent, despite the invitation to cut Taylor to ribbons.

That didn't bode well. Ever.

Some obscure emotion wound its way around her ankles, subtle enough, at first, that she wasn't sure what she'd stirred up. That mystery feeling became inescapable, squeezing and tightening its way up and up her body until it became an emotional anaconda that was squeezing the air out of her chest. *Trepidation, and a hell of a lot of it.*

She couldn't stand the constriction and loss of control, was so conditioned by fear to respond by shutting her mind down and focusing on surviving, that she almost missed the bright red mailbox denoting the road to the rental.

Taylor stomped on the truck's brakes, the back wheels chattering as she came to an abrupt stop. Backing up on the empty highway, she turned down the dirt road and passed under a black metal sign displaying the place's name.

Place. Ranch? Family? Resort? Whatever.

Losing control like that had left her too rattled to pay attention.

She pulled over, the truck's passenger wheels well into the pasture and, closing her eyes, let her head tip back onto the headrest. Doubt moved in, swift and assertive. Had she made a mistake coming here? Why did she think she could do this? What would happen to her if she couldn't? Clearly Monroe wasn't a compassionate man. Should she have booked someone else as her recertification guide? There were a handful of people she could have picked from, all of whom were qualified to see her through the process. There was no reason it had to be *him.* After all, he'd only just reemerged onto the climbing scene after more than a year's absence. It had been serendipity she'd tripped into a recommendation to Quinn Monroe from another climb instructor she'd contacted. That guy had been booked, but he'd told her Quinn was back in business, providing her with Quinn's new website and contact information. She hadn't been comfortable calling, scared he'd recognize her from the accident, which had made national news. Last thing she needed was to hear the derision or judgment that were bound to be in his voice. Rejection would be easier to take in an impersonal email.

She was wildly curious about him, though. No climber had ever worked so hard to gain international notoriety for his skill and then walked away from a career—with sponsorships—when he was at the top of his game. But Quinn had. And then he'd fallen off the grid. Two interviews had briefly featured him since then. In each, Quinn had refused to talk about the reason he'd quit. He'd been borderline surly in his responses when the interviewers tried to talk him around to discussing his stage-left exit. After all, they'd said, the climbing world wanted to know why.

Quinn's response? "The decision was driven by personal obligations, and I don't talk about my personal life. Sorry."

The last articles had been printed before the accident, but the dates were fuzzy. What she knew for certain was that Quinn had disappeared, closed up shop, not long after that. Maybe she should terminate the contract, find someone else.

Except he'd been the best. A person didn't lose that distinction simply because they took a hiatus. He'd voluntarily come back to the real-life Chutes and Ladders. She didn't need to know what prompted the absence or return, only that he was back and had the ability to lead her back, as well. To that end, she needed the best climber and instructor money could buy. So what if he'd never be nominated for Most Congenial Mountain Man? Heaven and hell alike knew that personality wouldn't save a person's ass in a pinch. Cold, logical decisions were their only chance.

"Looks like I'm keeping him," she whispered.

The admission didn't subdue her offended independence

and female pride. His gall chafed that part of her raw. Who the hell did he think he was, ordering her around as if she were some green climber who needed him to dictate her every move from the moment she hit town to the second she was off the mountain and on her way home.

What. An. Ass.

Of course, she hadn't exactly been a peach. More like a pit. She laughed, lifted her head and gasped as the view out the windshield hijacked her attention. Every bit of it.

A series of mesas ran north to south, their varying heights accentuated by extremely flat tops. Each mesa was a mélange of browns and greens, the grass a short carpet interrupted by cedar shrubs and split by the dirt road that snaked its way deeper into the heart of the ranch. At the foot of the nearest mesa stood a lone windmill. Cattle gathered around the stock tank below the spinning fan, their white faces and rusty-red-brown bodies bright against the neutral background of grassland. And above it all rose an endless blue sky.

Taylor shut her truck off and got out, walking to the front and leaning against the bumper. A slight breeze lifted tendrils of hair off her neck and cooled the shirt that sweat had glued to her skin earlier. Inside, she quieted, the change startling enough to be apparent but reality too big to be bothered by it. Never had she experienced anything like this. The mountains in Washington were big, but the space here?

Massive.

This wasn't the first time nature had made her feel small in relation, but this? No way was this the same. Standing there looking out over the wide-open space, the horizon appeared endless, the sky infinite.

All the questions that had been jockeying for position, each wanting her immediate attention, stopped. And Taylor breathed. Simply…breathed. Lungful after lungful she reveled in the clean air infused with earth and cedar and green growing things.

If a soul could sigh, she swore hers did.

Tires hummed on pavement, the sound carried by the wind. Unwilling to compromise the quiet she'd discovered, she got back in her truck, started it up and put it in Drive. She didn't look back.

The truck rattled and chattered all the way across the metal-pipe cattle guard.

"Rustic rumble strips," she mused.

The road was in very good shape, devoid of the washboard surface or shin-deep ruts inherent to dirt roads exposed to wind and rain. A good drainage ditch had been cut down one side. Fences were in good shape. Grass was grazed but pastures were clearly managed for conservation. She slowed as she reached the first incline. The herd stood spread out across the road like giant yard art, unmoving save for the occasional flick of a tail or slow, considering blinks of long-lashed eyes. They all looked young, given their size, but also healthy. And undisturbed.

She inched forward and the young cow—steer?— nearest her ambled off with a disgruntled chuff. The herd shifted around and a couple of others that had been in the road followed the first one out onto the grass.

Impatience bubbled to the surface and the urge to hurry things along got the best of her. Yes, the cows were moving, but they were too damn *slow*. Rolling her window down, Taylor waved an arm wildly and shouted. "Move!"

The cattle stopped and looked at her.

"Get out of the road!" she shouted.

She hit the truck's horn, *beep-beep-beep*ing before leaning on it hard and steady, the grating, obnoxious noise shattering the quiet.

One of the cows lay down. In the road.

The soul-deep peace she'd found was lost.

To a bovine antagonist.

"I've been reduced to this," she thought, tears and laughter arriving at the same time.

She gave in to both.

Several minutes passed before she even tried to collect herself. Several more passed before she was successful. Drying her face on her shirt hem, she fished around in the console for a napkin, blew her nose and tried to decide what to do. She could attempt to drive around the animal, but the pasture on either side had cattle scattered about. She could nudge this guy and try to get him to move, but she didn't want to hurt him. *How fragile* are *cows?* She also didn't want to bang up her truck if it turned out the animal was more dent-proof than her vehicle.

When she was two seconds from throwing in the towel and calling the cabin owner for help, the cow stood up and moved on.

The universe was laughing. She could hear it.

Unwilling to waste any more time, she drove through the remaining animals—who all moved—as fast as she dared. The road went on long enough that she wondered if she'd taken a wrong turn, and she crossed three more cattle guards before she rounded the mesa and found herself in a canyon and following a stream. Aspens clustered here and there, white trunks stark against the hillside, their leaves shimmering in the slight breeze. The stream widened and turned north, winding through an empty field littered with wildflowers.

A little house sat straight ahead. Other buildings were situated behind and, like the stream, to the north so they faced the water. She parked in front of the main house, put her hair back up and hopped out of her truck.

"It's like a fairy tale," she whispered, standing behind the open driver's door as if it would shield her from the fallout when the image shattered. And it had to shatter. Nothing like this existed in real life.

The house was half stacked river stone, half rough-hewn log cabin topped by an aged tin roof and embraced by a deep, wraparound front porch with tree branches used as porch railings. A porch swing hung from the rafters on one side while rocking chairs occupied the other. Country music played on a radio inside and, somewhere in the house, a woman sang along. The smell of fresh-baked bread drifted out of open windows. Beneath that hovered the scent of something rich and savory.

Please, God, let that be dinner.

Taylor laid her hand over her stomach when it growled in protest. When had she last eaten? Breakfast in Colorado? Must have been.

Taking a deep breath, she stepped away from the truck and shut the door.

Inside, the singing stopped.

Seconds later, the front door opened and a lovely woman stepped out, a dishtowel in one hand. She looked to be in her midfifties. Long dark hair threaded with gray had been braided, but a few flyaways rebelled. Worn jeans, faded and slightly frayed from a hundred washings, hugged slim hips. Her dark T-shirt had a smudge of flour on one corner. Her gaze met Taylor's and each woman lifted a hand in greeting and smiled at the same time.

The older woman laughed. "If you're Taylor Williams or if you're selling Girl Scout cookies, come on in. Otherwise, I don't need any, want any, have already registered to vote, found the Lord decades ago so He's not missing anymore and I'll warn you I have a loaded shotgun inside the doorway."

Taylor paused halfway up the front steps. "Shotgun?"

The woman's grin widened. "It's reserved for salesmen and politicians." She stepped forward, hand outstretched. "I'm Elaine Bradley."

A vehicle came around the bend. Taylor turned and squinted into the bright afternoon sun glaring off the windshield of what turned out to be a truck.

Light glinted off the late-model hood as it approached the house at speed. Slowing just outside of what Taylor considered the driveway, the driver pulled in at an angle, the dust trail the truck had kicked up rolling forward and swallowing the vehicle. The driver waited for the majority of the dust to clear before stepping out. Hat settled low on his head, he gripped the front of the driver's door in one hand and the cab in the other, leaning into the V created between the two. His eyes narrowed and the cords in his neck stood out.

"That's my son," Elaine said from behind Taylor.

No. No, no, no. This was not *happening.*

"Come on up and meet our guest," Elaine called out.

Taylor turned around and, clutching the step railing, swallowed hard. "*He's* your son?"

Merry eyes crinkled at the corners as the woman's smile widened. "He is, yes. Handsome as the devil is dark, and stubborn as a mule to boot, but he's a good man," she added softly, maternal pride coloring her words.

Heavy footsteps made the stair treads vibrate beneath Taylor's feet, stopping before the owner drew level with her. His presence loomed at her back, large and hot and strong. Déjà vu struck her and she almost laughed at the irony when the bourbon-smooth voice spoke into her ear.

"I'm sure there's a very good reason you're standing here, on my porch, on my land, talking to my mother."

His tone wasn't hostile but it sure as hell wasn't welcoming, either.

"Mind yourself, Quinn," Elaine bit out. "Taylor Williams is a guest of the ranch."

"I can't…" Taylor shook her head and stepped aside in an attempt to create space between her and the man at her back.

Quinn Monroe.

She'd thought this place was a fairy tale when she'd arrived—too pretty, too perfect, too good to be true. The thing was, all of the original fairy tales had been told as warnings. With this being Quinn's territory, that made him either the hero or the ogre. If she had to put money on which was more likely, he wouldn't end up king of the castle.

Fairy tale, indeed.

"GUEST OF…" QUINN was rooted to the spot. All he could think was that she was here and her damn hair was still up. "Since when?"

"Since I rented her the bunkhouse last week." His mom stepped to the edge of the porch and towered over him, her gaze boring into his in that parental way that brooked no argument. "You're well aware I've been working to revamp it, from décor to the new septic system. My intent was to make it available as a rental for people visiting the area, so once we were done, I listed it on a couple of online vacation-rental sites. Is there a problem?"

He had clenched his teeth so hard he wondered if they'd cold-welded. "You didn't mention that was your end goal, *Mom.*"

"Wait. You're a Monroe," Taylor interjected, looking at Quinn. "And Elaine, you're a Bradley?"

"Quinn's father and I split right after Quinn was born.

I married Alan Bradley before Quinn was two, and Alan raised him," she answered, not taking her eyes off Quinn. "When you treat me like an actual business partner, *son*—" and no one missed the emphasis there "—I'll reciprocate. Seems there's something going on you're not sharing yourself."

She snorted and flipped her dishtowel over her shoulder, shaking her head. "This isn't an argument we need to expose Ms. Taylor to." As she shifted her attention to Taylor, her smile returned. "I'm truly glad you chose the Rocking-B Ranch for your stay. The cabin, formerly our cowboys' bunkhouse, is about two hundred yards north with the barn situated just beyond it. It's a lovely two-bedroom place built as a smaller version of the main house. The porch there is much closer to the stream, so you can leave the windows open and listen to the running water if it suits. Above all, it affords you—" she glared at Quinn "—privacy. I'll walk you over now, if you're ready. Quinn, be a gentleman and grab her bags."

Taylor didn't look at him, didn't even seem to look at his mom when she spoke. Her voice was shaky but resolute. "I'm sorry, Mrs. Bradley. Given my unanticipated acquaintance with Quinn, I'm going to have to find another place to stay."

His mother glanced between him and the woman. "I'm not sure I understand."

Quinn rolled his shoulders. "She's my client."

His mother's eyes flared wide with alarm. "You're climbing again."

His answer was a single nod. No, he hadn't told his mother about Taylor hiring him to see her through recertification. He hadn't wanted to admit he'd been forced to lean on his former profession to shore up their financials. Cattle prices were lean this year, and the first three semi-truckloads of yearlings they'd sent to the sale had averaged a paltry seventy-nine cents per pound. If the remaining three truckloads did the same, the ranch would break even, covering operating costs and land taxes. There'd be nothing left over, nothing to live on.

Not to mention the bank note that had come due.

Quinn pulled his cowboy hat off and slapped it against his thigh. Sweat beaded on his nape at the memory of the notice that had come on official letterhead via certified mail. The ranch's operating loan was more than ninety days past due. They had thirty days to bring that loan current or the foreclosure process would begin.

He and his mother had put their heads together, trying to come up with some feasible option to raise the money. Short of selling off the equipment, which they needed, or the animals, which were their only source of income at the moment, they'd come up with nothing together—but, apparently, separate plans they hadn't shared with each other.

And Murphy's Law said those individual plans would involve the same woman.

He met and held his mom's unblinking stare. "Private discussion." The last thing he wanted Taylor to know was that he was desperate for her fee. It would undermine his authority, both in prep work and on the climb.

"Obviously communication isn't a strong point between me and Mom, but it doesn't change the fact you need somewhere to stay while we do the pre-climb work and then get your climb hours in." She started to object, and he interrupted in a rush. "Truly, Taylor. It's fine." Before she could argue, he tipped his hat and spun on his heel, strode to the Toyota and stopped at the driver's-side rear door. "Is it unlocked?"

Taylor looked at him, her face blank. "Your mom has

a shotgun. I think she's more a deterrent to thieves than the factory alarm."

Quinn grinned and pulled the door open, hauling out one moderate suitcase and a small overnight bag. He looked in the truck bed and found three decent-sized army duffels. "That all your gear?" He shook his head. "Never mind. We'll inventory what you brought later. I'll bring those over after a while."

"No worries." Taylor's voice was softer when she moved closer to Elaine, but Quinn heard her just fine. "You realize my staying here will be awkward, at best, and impossible, at worst."

Elaine shrugged. "Your options in town are the six-room motel run by the Moots. He's eighty-seven. She's eighty-six. The motel was renovated in 1958. No wi-fi, no cable and no kitchenette. You could check out the dude ranch to the south, but last I heard, they were booked through Valentine's Day next year. Beyond that? There's nothing else within sixty miles."

Quinn watched as Taylor worried her bottom lip with her teeth, rocking back and forth on her feet, sneaking looks between the truck and the general direction of the cabin. She settled her focus on Elaine. "I need to speak to Quinn, if you don't mind."

The woman gave a short nod. "I'll go in and wrap up the last of dinner. Holler when you're ready and I'll walk you to the cabin."

Taylor's smile was small and decidedly noncommittal.

Quinn hoisted her bags over one shoulder and retrieved one duffel, watching as Elaine disappeared into the house and Taylor skipped down the porch steps. He waited, watching her close the distance between them.

"Would you put those back in the truck, please? I need to talk to you."

He didn't comment but dropped the duffel at his feet and set her two personal bags atop the military-green canvas. He had a good idea which punch she'd throw first, but knowing wasn't going to make it any less painful. So he decided to swing first. "I'm going to go out on a limb here and guess that you're irritated."

Her flat stare was answer enough.

"Care to elaborate?"

She pulled her ponytail down, worked her hands through the loose curls and pulled the entire mass up in a sloppy topknot. "How long have you been running the ranch?"

"Coming up on two years too soon." Instinct shouted at him to proceed with caution. "Why?"

"Did you give up climbing for this?"

"Excuse me?"

"I want to know what your priorities are. If you're a rancher, you're a rancher. That's fine. But I didn't hire a rancher to see me through my recertification. I hired you under the express belief you were a dedicated mountaineer."

Muscles along his jaw worked and knotted. "I'm perfectly capable of doing, and being, both."

"I disagree." She crossed her arms and looked at some point well beyond him. "When was the last time you summited, Quinn? Eight months? Twelve? More?" She waved him off when he started to answer. "What you've been doing with yourself over the last several months may not matter so much to you, but it matters very much to *me*. I decided to hire you, signed the contract you required, paid your well-above-the-going-rate fee up front and then came *to you*, and I did it all based on your skills and qualifications as I understood them."

"And? I'm not tracking here, Taylor." He leaned one

hip against the rear door of her quad-cab pickup and mimicked her, crossing his arms over his chest. "If this is about the cabin rental, it's not that big a deal. The arrangement caught me off guard, but it'll be fine—easier, even, since I intended to have you come out here every day to train, anyway."

Her lips thinned. "This isn't about the cabin."

"Then break it down for me. Why, exactly, can't I ranch and climb? Is there some cosmic law that says a man is capable of one but never both?" he demanded, words razor sharp.

"I'm sure you can do both and be good at both. But to be the best at something, you have to focus, dedicate yourself and give your complete time and attention to that one thing."

His chin rose slowly until narrowed green eyes met her hazel ones. Drawing a deep breath, then another, he worked to keep his tone level and his hands from shaking. "That may be the most screwed-up logic I've ever heard. It's like saying a man can't be a CEO and a father."

The corners of her eyes tightened and she looked away. "Yeah? Well you hit that nail square on the head," she muttered, carrying on before he could question her. "For a man to be the best CEO, he has to dedicate himself wholly to that pursuit. He can't shut it off when he gets home and give the same time and focus to being a father." She met his gaze, then. "The demands of the CEO are always there, always hovering and commanding his attention, even as his kid does the same. Sure, he can give a percentage of his attention to one and the remaining percentage to the other, but he can't give his full time and attention to both, and never at the same time. And just because he's a father doesn't mean he's not a CEO and vice versa. So he's forever divided and only half as good as he might have been if he'd dedicated himself wholly to only one pursuit."

"I disagree." Anxiety, as unfamiliar as it was unwelcome, created distinctive half-moons of sweat under his arms. He instinctively picked up her suitcase when she reached for it and tried to check his panic. "I'll carry this for you."

"No need. I'm not staying."

He froze. This wasn't happening. Quinn needed this climb too bad for her to bail on him now. No, the climb wasn't what he needed. It was the fee. If she walked, he'd have to refund at least half the money she'd paid him based on the contract she'd referenced—the contract *he* had drafted. That couldn't happen, in large part because he'd spent two-thirds of it to settle the vet's bill for vaccinating the weanlings. There was no money *to* return.

"If you'll move your foot, I'll grab my gear and get out of your way."

He looked down, confused. "My foot."

"You're standing on my duffel handle."

Something in him snapped, and he ground his boot—and the handle—into the dirt. "So that's it. You track me down, hire me, show up and take one look around before deciding I'm not focused or dedicated or single-minded enough to be damn good at what I do." He leaned into her space, closing the distance until they were nearly nose to nose. "Who the hell do you think you are, putting me through the front-end work of interviewing you, checking references and all that shit only to have you show up and immediately declare me 'unfit' just because you don't like the backdrop I'm standing against? Is that your MO, Taylor, to pick and choose only what agrees with your definition of the world and deny everything, and everyone, else?" His eyes widened as hers narrowed. "Wow. Okay, fine. If you're that willing to quit before your first day of ground work, it's probably a good thing you've put on the brakes." He stepped back and picked up her duffel, tossed it in the bed of her truck and started for the house.

"I'm not quitting," she called after him with open defiance. "And it's my right to put on the brakes."

"Sure it is. It's just…" He waved her off. "Never mind. Best of luck to you."

"Just what?" she demanded.

"I've never once had someone with a quitter's attitude complete my groundwork let alone make it up the mountain, and trust me, Taylor. This is a quitter's attitude no matter how you dress it up." Quinn didn't slow or turn back when he delivered the kill shot. "You didn't stand a chance of passing the re-cert. This saves us both the embarrassment—you from failing and me from failing you."

4

He...did...not...

Taylor took off after Quinn, yanking on his arm hard enough he was forced to face her. "What?" he bit out.

"How *dare* you call me out for quitting," she spat. "You don't know me."

"I know you about as well as you know me, darling. I'd be willing to amend my opinion, though."

She waited.

One corner of his mouth kicked up. "I'd add that you're a quitter riddled with hypocrisy, coming down here and dishing out judgment on a stranger and then getting your back up when he does a little of the same in return."

Stepping into his space, she was forced to tilt her chin up and arch her neck in order to see him. "You don't get to make those allegations, not about me and never to me. Ever."

"Too late to warn me off, seeing as I just did." He waved her away. "Get in your truck and head back to wherever you came from. I have no doubt you'll be able to find someone willing to sign off on your paperwork for the right price. People like you seem to always have some kind of contingency plan."

"Wait. 'People like me.' Sounds a little like a snap judgment there, Quinn." The taunt hung there, suspended between them.

He didn't comment.

"I have to have this recertification, but I fully intend to earn it. I don't buy my way out of tight spots or life's inconveniences, thanks." He was right. Her back was up. She knew it. But this man pushed every button she had and accused her of all sorts of asinine stuff, to boot.

To say she'd buy her recertification...

First lesson dear old Dad taught me—achieve your goal, no matter what it takes or who you have to pay off.

Not a lesson she intended to employ.

The problem she faced was getting the recertification before her official post-accident medical leave expired. If she didn't report for duty by that date, certification in hand, her job-protected leave would expire. The unit would have to open her job up to outside applicants and fill the position. She wouldn't be guaranteed a spot.

Crap.

Taylor took a step away from Quinn and was struck nearly dumb at the realization that the man in front of her represented her best, and possibly only, shot at achieving her end goal. It changed things, and while she loved the idea of walking away under the power of moral superiority, that was so not going to happen. Truth? She had to decide whether she'd take her serving of crow with hot sauce or gravy, because one way or another, she was going to have to eat it.

Man, she hated crow.

Swallowing her pride and ignoring the bitter aftertaste, she squared her shoulders and met Quinn's bold stare with one of her own, fabricated as it was. "You know what?

Fine. I need this climb and I don't have time to organize another instructor."

"Flatter me much more and I'll lay prostrate at your feet begging for a belly rub." His tone and affectation were dryer than July dust, but he eked out a smile.

She cringed a little, realizing how bad her word choice had been. "Sorry." Drawing a deep breath, she held it and then let it out in a rush. "Look, I'd really like to start over. From the point I drove into town and encountered Old Joe and his mountain of chili, this has been a cluster." Shoving her hands in her pockets, she rocked back on her heels and forced herself to continue to meet Quinn's unblinking eyes. On a whim, she held out her hand and waited while he considered her offering. With a casual flair she could only hope to master someday, he took her proffered hand.

She smiled, more with relief than anything. "Hi. My name's Taylor Williams. I'm a Taurus, which explains my occasional superiority complex. The guy who read my palm for five bucks at the county fair assured me that I'm very fortunate my superiority complex is countered by both my humor and good taste. I consider picking out my toenail color a major commitment every time I get a pedicure. I rent my home, don't own. Maybe someday. I love baseball, cars, travel and camping, though not necessarily in that order. I will never put vegetables on my pizza because, really? That's just wrong. And I am absolutely willing to try anything once."

"Except veggies on your pizza," Quinn added.

She gave a mock shudder. "I did try it once. That's how I know what an extreme level of wrong we're talking about here."

He grinned then, wide and genuine, and her heart skipped in her chest when he squeezed her hand, which he was still holding. "My name's Quinn Monroe. I'm a Sagittarius and only know that because the newspaper horoscope says my birthday falls on that sign. I have no idea what that means about my personality, but I know myself well enough to know I'm honest, practical, hardworking, appreciate humor and I'm loyal to a fault.

"I love a good steak and will have a mild seizure if you put curry anywhere near my plate. Trucks over cars unless you're talking a 1969 Camaro Rally Sport. Then? This grown man will be reduced to tears, grunts of approval and inappropriate sounds of pleasure—all with the engine's first rumble. I prefer outdoors to in, believe towels should always be dried without dryer sheets and can't plow a straight line even if the tractor is equipped with GPS and the new self-drive technology.

"My cosmic gripe is that Brussels sprouts aren't sprouts but actually minicabbages. Some politician somewhere needs to make that part of his platform—Sprout Reform—because if the American farmer can't be truthful about his crop, and grocers perpetuate the lie, then the world has gone to hell and we're all just along for the ride."

Taylor found herself smiling before Quinn had finished his short monologue-slash-introduction, but the sprout rant? That tipped her over into full-blown laughter. Squeezing his work-roughened hand, she let go. "Sprouts are clearly a hot-button issue for you."

"You have no idea."

She nodded. "Clearly." She looked in the direction of the cabin, trying to figure out how to mend that last breach and put herself back on track. She wasn't entirely confident Quinn was the right instructor to see her through this, not with her complicated history and the voice of her father delivering one of an infinite number of stern speeches on the fact she needed to choose her life's calling and pursue it with singular focus. He'd raised her under the strict decree that an individual devoted his life to the pursuit of professional perfection in one thing and one thing only. To do otherwise was to divide one's focus and settle for being no more than half as good. He'd taught her firsthand, too, devoting himself to his profession before his family and, specifically, before his children.

Unwelcome doubt crowded her newfound relief. What if Quinn wasn't the "best" anymore? What if he'd lost the edge that made him a force on the mountain, notorious for taking calculated risks? What if he'd divided his focus and would only get her halfway to where she needed to be? What if—

The man occupying her thoughts interrupted her rapidly developing case of What-if-itis, tipping his head toward her bag. "Why don't I take these to the cabin and see you settled."

She grabbed her small suitcase and overnight bag, hoisted them over her shoulders and fought the surge of panic that struck without warning. To take that first physical step toward the cabin meant more than staying. It meant she would climb, putting her safety, her well-being, her *life* into the hands of the man before her.

He simplified things when he hefted the duffels containing her gear and grabbed her small ice chest. "I'll leave your rope duffel in the truck. We won't need them, even on the official climb. I prefer to use my stuff. Once you're settled, we'll work out our training plan. I want you to be comfortable with the approach I intend to use in recertifying you."

She swallowed hard and nodded, grateful she could breathe after finding she was unable to force sound around the fear clogging her throat.

If I stay, I climb.

He started up a narrow path, calling back, "Cabin's this way."

Her feet moved of their own volition, ultimately following him down the path. Looked like she was staying.

They made their way to the cabin and it took Taylor two-point-six seconds to fall in love. More cottage than true cabin, the rustic place was, essentially, a smaller version of the main house, from building materials to the wraparound porch to the stone chimney on one side.

Impossible as it seemed, the inside of the little house was more appealing than the outside with its warm-colored wood walls and floors, worn leather furniture huddled around the large hearth and the bright efficiency kitchen. Simple décor centered around the ranch's heritage, from pictures to tools to an old copper double boiler that had been artfully filled with dried wildflowers and displayed on the steps leading upstairs.

Taylor gestured to the loft. "Second bedroom?"

"And a three-quarter en suite bath."

"Your mom's seriously not charging enough per night," Taylor said, delighted. "But I'm selfishly glad." Moving into the bedroom on the main level, she dropped her bags on the floor beside the closet.

"I'm going to go out on a limb here and guess that Mom's got you coming up for breakfast and dinner. Breakfast is on the table at 6:30 every morning and dinner's around 6:30 every evening. Bring an appetite—she's a helluva good cook. Lunch is usually whatever we have lying around—leftovers or sandwich makings or some combination of the two." Quinn pulled his hat off and ran a hand through his hair. "I'll, uh, leave you to get settled."

He was gone before Taylor could protest.

She was alone.

Wandering through the space that would be hers for the

next couple of weeks, she looked in cabinets, checked out the loft and searched for extra supplies like paper goods, laundry detergent, dishwashing soap. It was all there. After opening most of the windows on the main floor, she grabbed a soda from the stocked fridge and headed to the living room. She lay down on the leather sofa and stretched out, tilting her head over the rolled arm. Overhead, ceiling fans whirred and rocked as they lazily stirred the cool afternoon breeze. She placed the as-yet unopened can against her neck. That extra burst of cold felt good.

Exhaustion stole over her and made her eyes feel gritty, her eyelids heavy and her limbs leaden. Setting the unopened can on the floor beside her, she rolled over with her back to the room and snuggled into the sofa. Her breathing slowed. The urge to close her eyes was too strong. She'd close them for a few minutes. Then she'd get busy, unpacking and showering before dinner. All she needed was…a…minute…

"FIRST RULE OF ranch *life*? Respect the ranch *wife*."

The words registered in her sleep-addled mind in a vague way. That voice—the one that made her imagine soft sheets, bare skin exposed to masterful fingers and whispered temptations in the dark of night—rolled through her, and her thighs clenched tight. Late-day sunlight glowed bright through her closed eyes. Warm afternoon light combined with the rush of consciousness to burn her dreams off as if they were little more than vapor. Awareness zipped over her skin. Every muscle in her body stiffened in a rush. And she fell off the sofa.

Scrambling to her feet, she scrubbed her hands over her face. "Why are you here? Did I oversleep?" Lowering her hands, she blinked owlishly at the owner of that voice. "Wait. How did you get in here?" She waved him off when the breeze carried the smell of food to her. "Forget it. Tell me I didn't oversleep."

The resulting deep chuckle was rusty but delicious. "Can't do it without lying, and I prefer to deal in truths."

She groaned and flopped onto the sofa, slouching as she draped her arm over her face. "Always?"

"Pretty much, unless there's a good reason not to."

Yep, he was smiling. She could hear it. "What constitutes a good reason?"

"Depends."

"On?"

"If you're going to chew my ass because you missed dinner, I'll lie through my teeth and tell you whatever it is that'll get me out of here the fastest and with the least damage."

"Chicken." But she smiled when she said it. Lowering her arm, she peered at him. "You really brought me dinner?"

He shifted, looking thoroughly uncomfortable. "Yep."

She lowered her arm another inch. "Why?"

He arched a brow. "Why what?"

"This is like a bad remake of 'Who's on First.'" Sinking lower into the sofa, she tried to ignore the sensual draw she felt toward the man, the draw that confused as much as it aroused. "Why did you bring me dinner?"

"It seemed like the neighborly thing to do."

She sat up, leaning forward and settling her elbows on her knees. "Why?"

He retreated to the kitchen and set the loaded plastic grocery bag he carried on the table. "I put everything in individual containers so you can eat what you want and save the rest for lunchtime foraging like we discussed." He pulled out container after container, pausing to wave one at her. "This is banana cream pie—best in the Southwest. Brought you an extra piece for good measure."

"You had me at pie. Then you said banana, and I became your slave."

That rusty chuckle again, saturated with amusement. "Good to know what your price is." He turned toward the door. "Call up to the house if you need anything. There's a two-way radio next to the phone. They're more reliable than cell phones out here."

It struck her as she watched him move toward the door that she didn't want him to leave. The realization was a complete sucker punch. She had an inexplicable urge to hear him laugh again—laugh until the sound wasn't so obviously unfamiliar to him. But for him to laugh, and for her to hear it, he needed to stay. Not *stay* stay, just not go. "Quinn?"

He paused but didn't turn around, didn't look at her.

She let out a breath she hadn't realized she'd been holding. "Never mind."

Quinn rolled his shoulders and crossed his arms over his chest. "About that." Allowing his arms to fall to his sides, he shifted enough to offer her his profile before clearing his throat. "I owe you an apology."

"No, you don't. If anything, I should apologize to you."

Quinn propped one hip on the counter. "We went over this earlier, Taylor. I was…well. Hmm. I want to clear the air and start fresh."

"We did," she said, nodding. "But the cloudy air was my doing."

"Let's agree to disagree and move on, Taylor. I don't want this to be something we argue over, okay?"

"Okay," she said with quiet acquiescence. Relief, albeit momentary, settled over her.

Maybe, just maybe, they could work this out.

QUINN RARELY DELVED into the emotional side of his life. Hell, *rarely* was actually more like *never*. It was foreign territory, somewhere he didn't go. So wandering around there with Taylor, a virtual stranger, left him out of sorts.

Struggling to find his balance, both in the situation and with the woman, he asked the first question that came to mind. "When did you start climbing?"

She blinked up at him, obviously caught off guard. "I, uh…" She shook her head and laughed, the sound slightly self-deprecating. "Last thing I thought you'd ask."

"What would've been the first?"

A shadow passed over her face, piquing his curiosity, but the pallor that followed and settled over her cheeks told him he'd hit on something significant. "Maybe later."

He shrugged with feigned nonchalance. "Tell me about your first climb, then."

"I summited on my first climb, though it was admittedly an easy attempt. I was fifteen." She picked at a loose thread on her shirt and didn't look up when she elaborated on her answer. "It was a stupid thing, really. Our family vacation was to the West Coast, and I was hell-bent on doing something different. I used my allowance to hire a beginner's guide."

"Hefty allowance."

She shrugged, dismissing the observation. "I saved." Then she looked up and smiled, the move changing the entire disposition of her face. "One of the best investments I've ever made."

Quinn had to clear his throat for his voice to come out as more than an approving grunt. *I've gone Neanderthal. Great.* "So, I take it you liked it?"

Taylor shook her head. "No. I didn't like it. I *loved* it. For the first time in my life, I was free. My well-being, my very survival was in my hands and the hands of my belay partner. I was free from the confines of..." Her voice faded even as her gaze darted away again. "Sounds pretty pathetic, I'm sure."

Quite the opposite, actually. He could relate, having found himself in the same spot, but at eleven years old, not fifteen. "The first time I set foot on a mountain with the sole intent to climb, I was lost to it. When I summited?" He grinned. "I swore I'd never come down. I was eleven. Turned out supper was a bigger impetus to a preteen boy than making a statement about his newfound love, and I ended up back home before dark."

She snorted. "I feel like a bit of a voyeur, getting such a personal glimpse into your life."

Quinn chuckled. "It's not too personal. The entire town watched me grow up and more than half were compelled to provide running commentary. There's never much privacy in a town this small. Someone's always got something to say about what you're doing or how you're doing it."

"What's it like, always having people around who know you or know what you've been up to?"

She appeared fascinated at the intimacies of living out here, so he went on to tell her more about his childhood and what ranch life was like, leaving out most of the hardships and sharing the high points.

Several anecdotes in, she held up her hand to stop him so she could catch the breath laughter had stolen. "Uncle. I'm calling uncle already. I can't take any more." Wiping her face, she shook her head. "It sounds wonderful."

"It had its moments," he admitted, surprising himself a little with the truth. Memories he'd dragged up and let roll around for fun caught him somewhere just behind his heart, and they shocked him. He'd never looked at his childhood like this, never recognized how much he'd been part of a home, not just on the ranch but in the county.

"Sounds like it was a great way to grow up."

He nodded, unable to put into words everything that rolled around inside his head...and heart. Instead, he slapped on his hat and nodded at her, touching the brim as a matter of courtesy. "I've got to finish up chores. The horses and our mammoth donkey, Cob, will be up at the gate ready for their dinner."

"Your donkey's name is Cob?" She looked up at Quinn, brow furrowed. "Is it because he eats corn cobs?"

The laugh surprised even Quinn, rolling up from deep inside him, a sound he hadn't issued since long before the funeral—an authentic, heartfelt, genuine laugh. Ignoring the way Taylor stared at him, he shook his head and rubbed his upper lip. "Cob got his name when he was born. C-o-b stands for cranky old bastard."

"And he got the name when he was a baby?"

"Sometimes animals, and people, are born as old souls. He was one of them." Quinn glanced at the door, the personal nature of the conversation making him antsy. "I'll need to get the stock fed and put up for the night before I can call it a day. My intent is to get started on your groundwork tomorrow after breakfast."

Her eyes widened. "Okay."

His internal barometer shifted, dropping into the Trouble's Brewing range. Shifting so he was square in front of her, though several feet away, he asked, "You okay with that plan or is there a problem?"

"It's fine," she blurted out, the words all but tumbling over each other.

"Okay," Quinn said. He needed to get out of here and gain some personal space and, with any luck, perspective. "I'll see you in the morning, then. G'night."

Flustered, Quinn pushed through the screen door, crossed the porch and took the cottage steps two at a time.

His booted feet hit the pathway with a *whump*. He didn't pause and definitely didn't look back. Rounding the corner of the house, he started across the field toward the barn and the last of his nightly chores. Not that bringing Taylor dinner had been a chore. He'd…enjoyed himself, had enjoyed chatting and talking about things he hadn't thought of in years.

Ahead, in the near dark, a horse nickered and the donkey's bray punctuated the greeting with a demand for food. After seeing to those animals he could hang up his hat and crawl into bed…where his mind would likely defy him and drag up Taylor's image.

Like it did now.

As Quinn walked between the cottage and the barn, twilight ceded to nightfall and shadows stretched and deepened, seemingly in time with each step that carried him farther away from the cottage.

From the surprising comfort he'd found.

From her.

His thoughts were a tangled mess. Images of Taylor mixed with sound bites and his wild thoughts until her face was the only thing he could truly focus on. Memories came in vivid color—denim, brown leather, dark chestnut hair—and were both new and unavoidable. Hardest to shake was the mental snapshot of her sleeping on that old sofa. It was in direct opposition to that raw flash of something—pain?—he'd seen only a few minutes later.

She'd been completely relaxed while she slept. He'd never seen her like that and had been enthralled, unable to look away. Long hair had tumbled around her shoulders and over the edge of the seat cushion. Long lashes had formed crescents over smudges of dark circles beneath her eyes—smudges he hadn't noticed before. Her slow, deep breathing hadn't faltered, her chest rising and falling in a soothing cadence as he watched.

Had she known he was there, it would have been different, and rightly so. But for that singular moment it simply was what it was. His pulse had slowed as his breathing self-regulated and matched hers. His muscles had gone lax. Nothing had sounded as good as curling up with her right then, and that, the very idea, jolted him out of the stupor he'd fallen into.

He'd stepped back, creating distance that had been absolutely insufficient. A hundred, even a thousand miles wouldn't have been enough right then. Waking her had seemed prudent, so he had, well aware he'd only been glossing over the momentary insanity that peaked with him wondering if her hair was as soft as it looked.

Her. Hair.

He was not, and never had been, that guy.

Lost in thought, he was surprised when he found himself making his way around a cedar tree.

Wait. There aren't cedar trees in this field. There aren't any trees in this field.

He looked up and shook his head in an attempt to scatter the swarm of thoughts that stalled out at the realization he'd walked past the barn. As in, he'd missed it. Completely. Looking around, he found that he'd inadvertently swung wide and passed the huge red building without even noticing it.

What…how…*what*?

He'd crossed every inch of this field as a kid, knew it like the back of his hand. How the hell had seeing a sleeping woman—a *client*, no less—turned him around so badly he apparently needed a flashlight and handheld GPS unit spitting directions at him to cross his own land?

Some guide I *am.*

Kicking a clump of grass, he backtracked to the barn, slipped inside and flipped the light on. Cob, the donkey—nay, jackass—and his equestrian gang were waiting at the pasture gate, huffing and stomping in wordless protest. Quinn let them into the barn and watched each animal go to his or her stall. They waited for him to close each door before continuing their opinionated communication on his late arrival.

"Hush, already. It won't be a habit, and you're far from starving." He chucked four hay flakes into the first feed bin, rubbed the horse's forehead and then moved to the next stall, repeating the act until he reached the stall nearest the big barn doors.

He reached out and stroked Cob's big, coffee-dark head as was his habit. Deep brown eyes considered him for a couple of minutes before the mammoth donkey flapped his lips and issued a half-hearted bray.

"I know, old man. I'm late."

Quinn pitched the hay flakes into the hay net, but Cob waited for his grain ration. The older animal almost pranced in place—his front half marching as his back half swayed—and eyed the old coffee can Quinn carried toward him.

"You know, I should probably cut you off. You've got a real problem here, my friend. If you'd act cool, not get so worked up over *food*, the horses would probably ask you to hang out more often." Which wasn't true. The horses were the ones pestering the old mammoth donkey for company, not the other way around. "It's like you're their quarterback."

Dumping the grain into the wall-mounted rubber bucket, Quinn dropped the tin can and ran a hand over the donkey's topknot and then moved to his ears. The animal's eyes drooped and his chewing slowed.

"Had the same thing happen to me earlier." The comment sounded loud in the barn's cavernous interior. "You have to watch those few souls who know how to rub just the right spots, Cob. They're the ones with the unspoken power to change things—to change *you*—and you're just fine the way you are. I mean, look around. You've got it made in the shade, my friend. Someone feeds you when you're hungry, you don't answer to anyone but have companionship when you want it, shelter from the literal storms and a support system for the figurative ones. Your life is your own, and…"

Quinn's words trailed off. He hadn't just described the donkey's life. He'd described his own.

In the silence of the barn, the life he described didn't sound quite so appealing but more like a cheap paint-by-number picture displayed in a custom, even ostentatious, frame. It wasn't at all free of the routine he'd always believed could, and would, become so rote that it ended up stripping a man of his ability to think on his feet. Nor did the impromptu sales pitch he'd delivered reveal a life lived to its fullest.

It sounded sad and more than a little lonely when he added the kernel of truth he'd left out of his assessment. As much as he enjoyed the woman's company, he needed her money.

And that, right there, was enough to shatter the illusion that he'd genuinely connected with another soul.

5

TAYLOR HESITATED ON the front porch, her gear in the two duffels at her feet and her helmet clipped to a belt loop at the back of her jeans. A light jacket might be wise, but she wouldn't need it long. The forecasted high would push ninety degrees with a fifty-percent chance of thunderstorms later in the day. Hard to believe given the mercury hovered in the midsixties right then. Humidity couldn't top thirty percent. The light breeze didn't help. But did she really need the jacket? She'd be working up a sweat within the hour. And…she was procrastinating.

"Shrug it off, Williams," she groused. Slipping on her sunglasses, she took a deep breath, flexed her hands and then hoisted her bags.

Her stomach growled. Breakfast hadn't been an option this morning, given the anxiety eating a hole in her stomach. Well, that and the fact she hadn't wanted to face off with Quinn. She'd sent Elaine a short text begging off today but promising to come up tomorrow and make the most of her hospitality.

"New personal boundary—no Quinn Monroe before 8:00 a.m. or after 7:00 p.m.," she muttered, and couldn't help but laugh.

Shifting the duffels to better distribute their weight, she veered off the path and headed across the field toward the barn.

No doubt the wood siding had once been a bright red. Time had done what it did best, fading the chipped paint to the point the color spoke of years long past, storms weathered and, through it all, shelter provided. The corrugated tin roof had lost most of its shine. The cupola perched at the roof's peak sported an aged copper weathervane covered in mottled verdigris. For all that the building appeared innocuous, it would be the site of more than one torture session as she put her body through its paces prepping to face two days on the mountain.

She hadn't climbed since... Throat tight, she forced herself to say it. "I haven't climbed since last May. Not since..." She coughed. "Not since the accident."

Sure, there had been exhaustive gym time spent getting back into shape, plus a few bike rides and more than half a dozen hikes. Not once had she been back to Mount Rainier, though. She'd had to force herself to shop for, and replace, her climbing gear. When she'd realized she would have to assess the damage done to what had been recovered from the accident, she'd simply replaced everything and thrown the box of old gear out without opening it.

Two nights before she left to come here, after indulging in wine-fueled fortification, she'd pulled all the new stuff out and geared up in her living room. She hadn't climbed, though. Not even the kitchen stepstool.

That changed today.

The nagging internal voice she had come to despise began whispering. Small things. Insignificant things. Things that weren't relevant to her odds of completing this morning's prep work. Those things evolved into worries and came one after another, tickling the back of her mind until they overflowed, their sheer volume threatening to drown out the rational voice she clung to. Her steps faltered and slowed.

Sweat slicked her skin, her shirt sticking to her back and shoulders. The long muscles on each side of her spine drew up tight, and her shoulders involuntarily hunched. She struggled under the weight of her gear. This seriously wasn't the way she'd envisioned the day starting.

"Stand there long enough and you'll grow roots."

Taylor nearly came out of her skin as Quinn strode past her carrying three duffels, not two. She straightened, chin lifted. *All the better to glare at you, my dear.* "If you're going to offer personal commentary, and I'm pretty sure you can't help yourself, at least pick something legitimate."

He spun around walking backward. "You're still standing there. I'd say that makes my assessment pretty valid."

She grabbed her bags and started after him. "I'm almost to the barn. If you're just passing me, it means it took you an entire field length to catch me. And *that* means I've been in front of you the majority of the time. Ergo? Invalid, or at least petty, complaint." She knew she sounded snarky, but the same tension that was drawing her shoulders toward her ears was sharpening the edge of every word that left her mouth.

"You actually use *ergo* in casual conversation?" He shook his head, a look of mock disappointment on his face. "So sad, Taylor. Five bucks says you were the nerdy kid who sat alone during elementary school lunch."

"I did not—" She stopped herself, then mimicked his look. "Poor guy. I get it now."

"Get what?" He wasn't faking the sudden look of wary distrust.

Good. She'd set him on edge. It was nice not to be

hanging out in that particularly dangerous mental neighborhood alone.

Brushing past him, she headed straight into the barn and made sure to bump the largest of his three bags, forcing him to shuffle in order to keep his balance. "You don't like to be challenged. You can't stand to lose face when you are challenged, because if you accept, which pride deems you must, you just might lose. And you don't like to lose, Mr. Monroe."

"Quinn, already." He crossed to an enormous climbing wall and dumped his gear. "For the record, I don't worry about challenges and don't hesitate to take them."

"Whatever you need to tell yourself to get through the day."

"I don't *lose*, Taylor," he said, grinning. "You'll learn."

That insidious voice in her mind laughed, the noise beating against her skull. She dropped one of her bags next to his and couldn't help but rub at the headache taking root behind her forehead. "No one wins all the time…Quinn."

He shrugged. "Maybe I'm the one who'll break that rule."

"Free advice? Unless you're just looking to give money away, don't bet more than five bucks on those odds." She dropped her other bag. "Ever." Her eyes adjusted to the dim interior and she squinted, trying to make sense of what she saw. Beside the commercial climbing wall, a metal monstrosity took up the entire corner of the barn. Vertical and horizontal pipes and beams of varying sizes were welded to a sturdy steel frame. Half again as wide as it was tall, the thing likely stood about thirty feet. Random small pipes stuck out, some as small as one-half inch around, while others were a solid foot in diameter. Some had small holes drilled through. No discernible order existed in size or placement. Nothing made sense.

Closer inspection revealed the whole thing was bolted at each corner to cement footers buried in the dirt. Within the frame were tracks, so the internal structure could be turned side to side as well as end over end. The entire thing looked like something hell's managers would install—a jungle gym of eternal damnation. Instructions? *Scramble around this thing while we spin it. Ready? Climb, monkey! Climb!* No doubt it would be effective as a means of punishment.

She reached up to push her hair out of her face, pausing halfway.

Climb.

Her stomach flipped over…and over again. Once wasn't sufficient given the dread washing through Taylor as she began to imagine exactly what this thing was for. Dots speckled her vision and she swayed where she stood. She could climb the thing. Probably. But climb and spin? He wouldn't. There was no reason to put her through that hell.

The sensation of falling, just like that first plunge on a rollercoaster, struck her hard.

Someone shouted. "We're going down!"

Her stomach lurched into her throat. Swallowing rapidly, she shook her head and found herself sitting on the barn floor.

Where the hell had that come from?

"Taylor?"

The statement held none of the judgment she would have expected. That had to be why she answered. "What is this thing?"

"A climbing simulator I built a few years ago when a sponsor of mine had me going to events for promotional purposes. It gives novices the experience of a more rigorous climb."

"And now it's in a barn."

He looked up and took in the metal behemoth. "I had it shipped down here when the promotional tour was over. Figured it might come in handy someday." He shot her a wide smile. "Turns out I was right. Again."

"Does it really turn?"

He nodded.

"How fast?"

He reached for her. "You're a little green."

"How fast?" she demanded, yanking her arm out of reach.

"It's a very slow revolution. I run the controls and won't let it get away from me. Also, you're strapped in, so you won't fall, if that's your concern."

"To what end?" she wheezed. Looking over, she found him considering her with open concern. "Why push a climber this way?"

"It encourages the climber to look for the next foothold, the next anchor point. The goal is to teach a climber to engage natural instinct and pair it with both common sense and experience to get the climber to trust the combination." He looked up at the contraption. "Instinct is rarely wrong."

Unless it's mine.

"This is where we're going to start. How well do you listen to your instincts, Taylor?"

She didn't need a metal torture device to answer that question.

A destroyed helicopter and seven dead men already had.

QUINN COULDN'T PUT the pieces of this woman together. She was obviously smart, competent, quick-witted and capable. Her climbing certifications had checked out and her background check was clean. She had a stable work history and incredible climb experience. But there had been these little glimpses, pieces of the puzzle that made her who she was, that contradicted the woman he knew—or *thought* he knew—her to be.

Like now.

She'd been bantering with him, a small bite in words that held no real heat. He liked that she kept him on his toes, that she didn't let him intimidate her. But she'd taken one look at his climbing machine, confirmed she'd be turned upside down and responded by executing an immediate ass-plant. What had scared her? And she would probably argue if he asserted she'd been scared, but he knew that look. He'd taken enough newbies up to know fear when he saw it. With her background, it shouldn't have shaken her.

He *hated* speculation.

More than that, he hated being reduced to a bystander in any given struggle. Being forced to watch as his mother grieved his dad's loss while he stood by and could do nothing to help her had been, by far, the hardest part of coming home. He couldn't fix it, and he wanted nothing more than to do just that. Hell, part of him *needed* to do it.

The same feelings were spurred on now, and he didn't like it. Taylor wasn't family. She wasn't a close friend. She was a client, not…more. Still, the urge to help her, to encourage her to find her way out of whatever darkness threatened to claim her—it pushed him with near physical force. Like it was instinct.

The word scalded his conscience.

Had he been living and working here, instead of chasing his dream of mountain climbing all over the world, that same instinct would have been in play when his dad had needed help. Quinn would have been the one to climb the windmill. He would have come down alive, gone home and had dinner with his parents. His dad never would have left the ground, never been high enough up to fall that far down. If Quinn had been here.

But he hadn't.

And seconds ago I stood here talking about engaging instinct and trusting it.

Lip service had never been his style, pretense had never looked good on him and hypocrisy left a seriously bitter aftertaste.

The way he saw it, he had two choices. He could put up or shut up.

Never in his life had he been able to shut up, which meant he really had one choice.

Taylor had closed her eyes before curling forward, wrapping her arms under her thighs and resting her chin on her knees. Getting her to meet him halfway required a level of trust he hadn't yet earned. It bugged him that she didn't seem to feel that same connection he'd felt. Not that that translated to trust, but it would have counted for something. Whatever the reason behind her hesitation, he needed to help her work past it.

A few steps forward brought him close enough to crouch in front of her. Balanced on the balls of his feet, he reached out and hooked a finger under her chin.

She twitched. Hard.

"Hey." He gently nudged her chin up. "Taylor? Look at me."

"Pass, thanks."

He stroked his thumb over her soft skin, back and forth in slow sweeps. "No can do."

"Try. I'm sure you have it in you."

Tweaking her chin, he rose, ignoring her muttered, "Told you so." He went to the tack room, not sure if she paid him any mind or not. According to her résumé, she hadn't started her search and rescue career on the ropes but on horseback. They'd be taking it old school this morning.

Quinn grabbed two halters with leads and, ignoring Taylor—who was definitely watching him—he left the barn without further comment. A sharp whistle got the small herd's attention. With their fearless leader, Cob, at the fore, the mammoth donkey and "his" horses came in at a lazy trot. Quinn shut the corral gate after the last animal passed through, then moved in among them. Big brown eyes watched with curious interest as he haltered Amante and Jigsaw, the two geldings he needed. He'd put the rest out to pasture later.

Cob made a hiccupping sound as his attention swung back and forth between his buddies hanging out in the corral and the two he clearly thought had been selected for an adventure.

"You coming, buddy?" Quinn grinned as the donkey flapped his lips and rolled his eyes. "Your choice. Stay or go." He opened the gate and stepped through, horses following, and that was it.

Adventure won.

Cob trotted through, braying loudly.

"You're either bragging or bitching. Either way, hush."

The four of them entered the barn, Cob in the lead. When the old animal saw Taylor, he stopped and brayed again, the sound resonating in the huge space.

Confusion flashed through Taylor's eyes before settling on Quinn's face. "What are you doing?"

He shrugged. "We're going to do this a little differently."

"Horseback."

"Yep." And, nope, he wasn't giving her a choice. "We ride with bits around here. You light-handed enough with the reins to manage your horse's soft mouth?"

Her gaze darted between him, the two horses, the braying donkey and the climbing contraption that had knocked her on her ass before he'd sent her up. "I'm not clear on how this is relevant to my recertification."

This was where he had to tread carefully. "You hired me, right?"

Her brows drew together. "To climb, yes. To ride horses? No."

He waved her answer off. "You hired me, but do you trust me?"

She wrapped her arms around her torso, her brows drawing even tighter. "What do you mean?"

There was that pang again. "You need to be able to answer in the affirmative before I'm willing to take you on a grade five climb, Taylor. I need to know—*you* need to know—that when I tell you to do something, it's in your best interest to do it."

"And you think I'm going to learn to trust you by going on a trail ride with you?" She laughed, the sound devoid of humor. "Wait, wait. Don't tell me you think the answer to establishing mutual trust is hidden in that fractional space between ass and saddle leather? No need to go all Zen on me now, Quinn. I need to get up the mountain and down so I can move on."

There was something there. She hadn't said she needed her recertification in order to get back to work. No, she'd said she needed to move on. "What is it you're moving on from, Taylor?"

Every ounce of color drained from her face. "There are so many things."

Quinn paused, hand on the saddle blanket. "Name the first two that come to mind."

Her head whipped around and she stared at him with hazel eyes gone oddly blank. "I want to live again, really live. I want to get up in the morning without the weight of regret making every step feel like I'm wearing cast-iron shoes." Her chin trembled.

"Sounds pretty hard to get up and put one foot in front of the other." He delivered the comment quietly, intentionally free of judgment, keeping his focus on the horse he was saddling up.

"It is." Her response was so strained he wondered that the words didn't shatter.

"What's the other one—the other thing you're moving on from?" Again, he didn't look at her.

The silence hung on long enough that he thought she wouldn't answer, but then her voice reached him, little more than a whisper. "I want to trust myself again."

"What happened that you don't trust yourself?" The quiet of the barn, with only the horses' whuffling, made the conversational lull feel heavy, and even heavier when she didn't answer. "Taylor?" He glanced over and went still.

She stood there, looking at the barn wall behind him, tears streaming down her face.

"Taylor?" he asked again, this time leaving the half-cinched saddle and moving toward her. He didn't think, simply pulled her into his embrace. Her lithe body was small against his, yet her every shudder was strong enough to rock him, forcing him to fight to keep his balance. "Let it go. Whatever it is, leave it right here."

The first hard sob ripped through her, and Quinn tightened his hold on her. "You won't come apart. Not while I'm holding on. Let it go, honey."

And she did, sobbing until her tears soaked his shirt through.

When she finally quieted, he loosened his grip a fraction.

She used that reprieve to wiggle out of his arms. Turning away, she lifted the hem of her shirt and scrubbed her face. "I'm sorry."

He watched her carefully, picking his way through the emotional minefield until he found a path forward. "For what?" Grabbing the cinch, he tightened it around the horse's girth and forced himself not to go plowing into Taylor's troubles.

"For what?" she asked on a near-hysterical laugh. "For falling apart all over you!"

"Pfft." He glanced over with a smile he made sure reached his eyes. "It's good for a guy's ego to feel he's useful, and my ego obviously needs the boost."

She did laugh then, and he fought with himself over whether or not to ask her about what had set her off.

Taylor settled his inner debate. "Thanks for not pressing me to talk it out. I've had about all of that I can stand."

"No problem." He handed her the reins to her mount's bridle. "You'll be riding Amante today. He's a sound horse, easy rider, and with your background and experience, still lively enough to be fun."

She took the reins without a word.

Quinn plucked his cowboy hat off the horn on Jigsaw's saddle and turned, leading them out of the barn. Time to cowboy up and be the kind of man he'd been raised to be—the kind who earned a woman's trust. They'd taken the first steps when she let loose the emotional purge that tore her apart.

He needed more from her, though. To make the climb, she'd have to trust him enough to tell him what it was that haunted her. Otherwise? That stuff could manifest on the mountain and put them both in jeopardy.

6

TAYLOR ADORED THE sweet-natured horse Quinn had paired her with, but she'd been head over heels in love with the tagalong donkey, Cob, before they were out of sight of the barn. The animal trotted ahead and then back, wagging his tail like a dog. He darted off the trail on occasion only to come haring back, eyes bright and expression impossibly cheerful. He would move in behind Quinn and try to pull the man's hat off. He even succeeded once, forcing Quinn to give chase.

She had no idea what Quinn was up to, requiring her to get on a horse and follow him around. They rode along in silence for about half an hour. He would occasionally point in a direction, and she'd look over to find he'd spotted a deer, an eagle or, once, an elk. The wildlife sightings fed into her earlier perception that this place was a real-life fairy tale, a world protected from the mundane ignorance and unnecessary violence that saturated everyday life, as twisted as the media painted it.

Cob splashed across a stream with obvious glee before heading up a short hill. Quinn and his flashy paint, Jigsaw, followed, while she and Amante, the chestnut-colored gelding, brought up the rear.

She couldn't keep silent any longer. "Tell me your plan isn't to follow a riderless donkey through the foothills."

Quinn twisted in his saddle, completely at ease, and pushed the brim of his hat up in order to make eye contact as he answered. Then he grinned. Not smiled. *Grinned.*

A loud shushing noise filled her head. Sparks flew, some internal and—she thought—some between them. Everything that had been running through her mind high-tailed it out of reach. Then her mental hardwiring short-circuited. Talk about being left at a disadvantage. If she had to do anything beyond stare, she was screwed. Okay, she could probably manage to drool. Might not even be able to stop herself.

No drooling, her pride admonished above the white noise that now roared between her ears.

She'd never seen him smile before. Not like this. Not in such a genuine way. Not when he appeared so relaxed, so comfortable, so thoroughly at ease. Not when he acted with kindness and a laid-back approach to whatever, or whoever, crossed his path. And certainly not when every word out of his mouth wasn't a teasing jab or sharp-tempered barb. Something about the way he appeared now screamed *This is the man behind the curtain!*

It was easy to understand that this place—land, community, animals, home and everything else that made up this pocket of the world—belonged to him as much as he did to it. The connection between man and land was almost tangible and impossible to miss. Above all, it made sense. She hadn't been able to reconcile the mountain man she'd expected with the cowboy she'd met, but that was then. This was now. Never had she realized the distance between two points of understanding could be so great.

Most surprising was that her newfound clarity soothed her heart and mind. He'd been absolutely right when he said he wasn't solely responsible for the way they'd clashed. Her preconceived ideas had colored her perceptions with primary colors, harsh and bright, when, in truth, he was made up of a thousand shades, from bright white to pitch black and everything in between. She'd cheated him in her estimation. Badly. And that changed things even more. Changed *her* in a fundamental way she wasn't willing to look at, no matter how small that change might be. Just then? The internal shift felt significant, an easy 6.2 on the emotional Richter scale.

I haven't known him long enough to pretend to know what makes him tick.

Her subconscious had a point, but that cynical voice couldn't gloss over what she'd recognized. Nor could it argue that the pieces her conscious mind had sorted out were a true representation of the man. This ranch, this land, this life—each part, each component, was a puzzle piece that helped her put together a more accurate picture of the type of man Quinn had been raised to become and the man he consequently was—the type of man her father would deem a "settler," as in, he settled for what he had and never strove for more, a man who was divided in his pursuits and therefore lacked true purpose. She had been raised to fear that approach to life, to view it as an insufficiency, a character defect.

Yet watching Quinn sit tall in the saddle, she couldn't see a single deficiency of form, value *or* character.

She was contemplating the man himself when he pulled up and waited for her and Amante to move within reach.

He claimed her horse's reins and said…something.

Taylor waved her hands as if clearing the air. "Wait. Got lost in thought. Say that again." She tried to take her horse's reins back to no avail.

Quinn held tight as he watched her. "Where'd you go?"

"I'm right here."

"Not what I meant, Taylor. You zoned out for a minute and thoughts were running across your face like subtitles, but I don't read that fast." The genuine concern in his eyes translated to the tone of his voice and elicited a deep response in kind from Taylor.

"I…uh…" She didn't know if it was based on Quinn's apparent concern or the fact that the question felt so earnest. "I've never seen you smile like that. Caught me off guard."

He pushed the brim of his hat even higher, revealing his furrowed brow. "So, I smiled and you mentally left the county."

More like the state. Or the region. "You shocked me. That's all."

"Okay, then." He cocked his head. "You've seen me smile before."

"Not like that," she answered below her breath, but with enough emphasis that he seemed to hear her.

With a short shake of his head, he dismounted and offered her a hand down.

She looked around. "Where are we going? Because this—" she gestured wide "—doesn't look like a destination."

"Funny thing about ranch life. We're sort of a finicky group when it comes to having touristy stuff parked in our pastures. For example, I could have a gravel lot and a hitching post installed here, add a few signs regarding the nature of the hike and the request that visitors make it on foot to preserve the landscape, but it just seems…" He paused and struck a dramatic pose, much like the bronze sculpture, The Thinker. But better looking. Then he popped up and grinned. "Stupid, since I much prefer it this way."

If he kept smiling like that and being so charming,

she was going to become his personal fast-food burger combo—he could have her any way he wanted her.

Taylor sucked in a lungful of air and choked, turning and all but scrambling away from the walking, talking, devastatingly appealing man she didn't understand and yet was beginning to want in the worst way. She could *not* believe she'd thought that, even to herself. Never had she been one to think about sex that way, let alone offer herself up, even mentally, like a fast-food meal.

She could deny it all she wanted, but the very thought sent images racing through her mind and heat blooming deep in her core.

Reduced to this by a smile and a relaxing day. I've been lonely too long.

And that, that last admission, was the one that finally knocked her off-center.

"Taylor?"

Stumbling to a stop, she glanced around and found Quinn twenty yards behind her, standing and holding his horse's reins. Cob was halfway between her and his cowboy.

"The trail I want to take is this way."

"Of course it is," she said under her breath, before calling out, "I'll be right there."

"Don't wander too far without Cob."

That forced her to face him. "Without the donkey."

"He's good safety out here if you're on foot."

She took in the shrubbery, foothills around the mountains, valleys and wide grassland behind them. "You don't expect to be waylaid by outlaws or attacked by bears or held hostage by crazed cattle intent on securing their freedom, surely."

He chuckled, leading the horses toward a felled cedar log that had metal rings driven deep into the wood. "We do have bears, but it's the mountain lions and coyotes I'm more inclined to worry about. The cattle? Well, I hadn't considered it, but I wouldn't suggest you approach them if you come across any. Those that are this far out see humans roughly once a year and tend to be a little squirrely as it is. And I'm the closest thing to an outlaw on the ranch, but I'm only a threat to…" He snapped his mouth shut and tied the horses up. "What I want to show you is this way."

She started toward him. "You're a threat to what, Quinn?"

"Nothing."

"Go on," she pressed as she passed the donkey and followed him up what she now recognized was a narrow trail. Not that she was watching it. The man in front of her had a seriously fine ass. *How did I miss that?* "Come on. Don't leave me hanging. What were you going to say?"

Broad shoulders stretched the soft cotton of his shirt when he shrugged. "Just being a smart-ass, Taylor. Let it go."

Not about to happen. "You mentioned trusting you when we were in the barn. This is part of that very thing, don't you think—telling me what's on your mind?"

He whipped around and, like he had outside the barn, walked backward so he could watch her. "Remember, you asked." Stopping on the path, he shook his head and smiled, the look unguarded and self-deprecating. "I was going to say that I'm the closest thing to an outlaw that the ranch has, but I'm only a threat to a good steak and an attractive woman."

She closed in on him and stopped a few feet away. "Seeing as we don't have a steak or campfire handy, and there's no one out here you might steal one from, your conscience is likely to remain clear. As for the pretty woman, there isn't one to tempt—"

He moved before she could make sense of what she saw. Closing in on her, he pressed three work-roughened fingers across her lips, gently, but with enough pressure to get her attention. "You're only half right in your thinking. No, I don't have a steak out here. Back at the house? Well, that's different. I'll likely throw a couple on the grill for dinner since Mom's gone into the city and won't be back for a couple days. That leaves me as the cook."

Her eyes flared impossibly wide. *Elaine. Gone for two days. Me, here. With Quinn. Unsupervised. And now he proves he can be courteous and smile. And he's hot as hell to my stone-cold heartache. This has more trouble written all over it than a country song.*

"As for the pretty woman?" He moved fractionally closer, let his fingers trail up her cheek and down, exposing her lips. "I'm qualified to say you've got that covered. In spades."

Her heart skipped a beat, sputtered and then began a wild, poorly executed solo version of the flamenco in her chest. "I'm not sure what I'm supposed to say to that. 'Thank you' doesn't seem quite right, given our relationship. Not that we *have* a relationship. Not like that. It's more, well, whatever it is... Shit. You know what I mean."

She popped her knuckles, a nervous habit she'd all but squashed. "It's just that thanking you would be appropriate if what you said was a genuine compliment, but we didn't start out like that. Saying nice things to each other, I mean. I'm shutting up now."

"While it's absolutely a genuine compliment, it's also a personal observation, so you don't need to say anything at all." Blinking rapidly, he seemed to snap back to his senses, dropping his hand and stepping away from her. The move created enough space between them that a truck could pass through without threatening anyone's toes. "C'mon."

Taylor followed him up the trail, her mind like a whiteboard that had been full of important calculations and notes and reminders before Quinn came along and wiped it clean. It had taken him a matter of minutes and no apparent effort. Yet he'd been complimentary in the process. A gentleman, even. What was she supposed to do with that?

Looked like she had nine days to find out.

QUINN FOLLOWED THE barely-there trail. The unexpected contact with Taylor, as well as the conversation that came of the tender touch, had rattled him straight through. The touch had been as unexpected as the conversation had been hoped for. He'd chosen to bring her to this spot based on the sole fact it was his favorite place on the ranch, the place he always came to if he needed to sort out his head when his reality grew too heavy or life became too complicated.

The moment at hand would add a third reason for his making the trek. He didn't know what else to do to create a touch point with a person who needed an intimate connection. Not intimate as in sex, though his mind raced down *that* path like it was Lewis to his body's Clark. The two would partner and make whatever sacrifices were necessary to draft an accurate topographical map of Taylor Williams, from head to toe. For the first time in his life, he found himself astounded at what testosterone could do to a grown man's common decency, not to mention his common sense.

What Quinn had actually been thinking fell more in line with establishing emotional intimacy, the type that created a sense of transparency and resulted in the knowledge a person was safe in the moment, as well as in the company he or she kept.

He fought the grimace that twisted his lips into a shape he didn't need to see in order to know it was fugly. *Look out, Dr. Phil. Your competition, Cowboy Quinn, is prepping for prime time. Right here. Right now. Lettin' all the emotions hang out.*

Yanking his hat off his head, he slapped it against his thigh. It bothered him that she'd confessed she wasn't sure how to take a simple, albeit genuine, compliment. Why? A woman like her, one who possessed that sexy inner fire and paired it with raw physical appeal, should stack up compliments like a bartender would shot glasses on a Friday night. That she'd been thrown...

Quinn glanced back at her and found she'd pulled her sunglasses off and now held them by one arm between her lips as she braided her long hair.

She caught him looking and tied the braid off a bit short. "I haven't fallen behind."

"You're fine." *Understatement.* He slowed a bit and waited for her to catch up, trying to think of the best way to get her to open up a little. Without his mental consent, his mouth opened the conversation with, "So, tell me a little about you."

"I answered all your questions on the application to hire you. Seems like you should have everything but my measurements," she said, shouldering him even as she teased him.

And now that's the question I can't stop thinking about. "I suppose the questionnaire is a bit...thorough."

"I understood why it needed to be," she added.

"I had a question about your application."

"You already agreed to take me up and I've paid half the fee." Desperation rang loud and clear through her every word.

He didn't get it, and he didn't know exactly how to lead into a conversation that might get her to open up. Everything he considered sounded completely wrong. He curled the edges of his hat, a lifelong habit he fell back into when he was thinking. Cob stepped in front of him and flicked his tail, so Quinn reached out and slapped the donkey on the butt. The move earned him a single, protesting *whoof*. "Get your ass in gear, Cob."

Taylor moved closer. "What kind of ass is he?"

"A big one."

The sound of her laughter was soft and bright, yet powerful enough that it rolled him without breaking a proverbial sweat. Worse, the wind had hardly carried the last note away before he found himself wanting to experience the whole of it again, her laugh, and it *had* been an experience. He wanted to hear the sound over and over so he could memorize the variable tones and call up the sound of her at will.

Cob stopped in the middle of the trail and forced Quinn to pass on one side and Taylor the other in order to keep moving.

She paused at the animal's head, resting her hand on his broad cheek and staring at him with a silly smile. "He seems like a sweetheart."

"He's not."

"You sound pretty sure of yourself, cowboy." She peered around the donkey's broad nose, the skepticism in her gaze one of amused irritation. "Your donkey here might beg to differ."

"He's actually a mischievous old man. Pampered, yes, but he's more a chips-and-beer guy than the champagne-and-caviar gentlemen his pedigree would have you believe."

Her lips twitched before she clamped them down into a hard line. "Which breed is he, exactly?"

C'mon, Williams. Don't lock down on me now. "He's a mammoth donkey. We, my family, used to joke that

Cob's Latin name should have been *Dumboicus Humoricus Crapsaloticus*, based on scientific fact."

"Pray tell."

Her mouth twitched. I saw it. "It's all legitimate. We founded his reclassification based on the size of his ears, his personality and the fact that he has created his own waste management crisis when it comes to mucking out stalls."

Her mouth did turn up then. Just a little, but it was undeniable. "And which brand of beer does he lean toward?"

"Michelob Ultra in the bottle."

She'd been petting that broad, velveteen muzzle but paused. "I would have taken him for a can man."

"Only way you'd find him with that turtle piss in hand, or hoof, would be if the apocalypse came and went, and the angels took all the good stuff with them when they beat wings back to heaven."

She smiled at the same time she worried her bottom lip with her teeth. An innocent move. No stratagem employed to get something from him.

He knew that.

Honest.

But knowing it didn't change the fact he considered it sexy as hell—the thought of teeth on sensitive skin—hers to his, his to hers, it didn't matter. *Salt from her skin would coat my tongue. Heat radiating from her body would scald my lips. Her tangled mass of hair would slip over her bare shoulders. I'd brush it away, those waves that cloaked her upper body, and reveal raspberry-colored nipples.*

Quinn was just getting into the naked part of his fantasy when Cob nudged him. Not hard, but with enough force, mammoth to man, to almost plant him on his rear in the dirt.

He tried to catch his breath but each inhale proved to

be the equivalent of bludgeoning his lungs, and each exhale left him lightheaded. The radical surge of blood to his groin defied any internal speed limit that logic might have imposed, the weight of his arousal suggesting lust had seized control of the wheelhouse and would go where it pleased. Apparently, that was straight to his cock. The damn thing needed a chaperone. And the rest of him could do with a little shock therapy, seeing as he'd obviously lost his mind.

After a subtle shift he was able to use the donkey's body to hide the telltale swell behind his zipper. Wrangler jeans were made to handle rough wear, but Quinn was pretty sure the company's quality control hadn't considered the possible need for in-the-field erection testing when they designed the iconic denim.

Cob looked over his shoulder, long ears wagging, and peered at Quinn with one big brown eye. After a few seconds, the jack blinked and nodded, the look on his face clear. *I expected more from you than this, hiding your irrepressible hard-on behind an ass. Funny, but not your finest hour, Walks on Two Legs.*

"Do *not* go *Dances with Wolves* on me," Quinn muttered. God save him, he was losing his mind.

Taylor leaned back and met Quinn's gaze. "Dances... with wolves. Care to explain that?"

He knew the look on his face was probably less than two degrees of separation from manic to call-the-white-coat-with-the-sedative-syringe crazy. Despite the thoughts he couldn't rein in, he offered her the only answer he could. The truth. "With the way things have been over the last year, maybe even year and a half, I'm not sure it's possible. Hell, I'd be willing to bet I could create a comprehensive PowerPoint presentation that represented the path my life took and the choices I made and Fate's intervention. I could incorporate color-coded pie charts and line graphs. I could also talk about metrics and data analysis and strategies until I lost my voice. I could even do it all while using a five-dollar-word, Ivy-league-ordained vocabulary. None of that would change the fact that the inside of my head is a strange hell no one could possibly understand."

Taylor leaned on Cob's back. "You could've just said no."

Talk about stripping the wind from a man's sails. "And you would've accepted that as an adequate answer?"

Her smile had altered course so it now headed toward more genuine. "Nope. Still won't. Tell me about this PowerPoint presentation." She waved a hand wide. "We've got time."

"Twenty Questions, is it?" he teased.

"I'm not putting myself on the line for twenty questions," she mused. "Three. Best I can do, but you have to answer, too. Same questions for each of us, and I go first."

"That'll give you two questions and me one."

She winked at him. "Then make yours count."

He grinned. "Make it four questions, two for each of us, and you're on."

"Deal, but I still go first." She tapped a finger against her lips, her eyes alight, and he saw the moment she decided on her first question. "Why do you still live at home?"

Quinn stared at her, mouth hanging open. "You have the world of questions at your fingertips and you want to know why I live at home."

She shrugged. "Sue me."

"I should," he muttered. "Fine. I live at home because it was convenient when I came back to Crooked Water."

She gave him a deadpan stare. "You know, this game

is going to be over in less than three minutes if that's all you're going to offer as an answer."

He rolled his eyes. "Fine. You want the down and dirty, just remember you'll be dishing the same."

She went dead still. "It's okay. That's fine, if that's all you want to tell me—"

"Nope. I'll answer and expect the same in kind." He pretended not to notice that familiar flash of fear cross her face. "A year and a half ago, my dad was killed in a ranching accident. He went up the windmill tower to fix a jammed fan. The sheriff thinks it broke away and the tail whipped around and caught him off guard. Knocked him…" He paused, took a deep breath. "Knocked him to the ground. He broke his neck on impact. They suspect his death was instant, so that's a relief." He paused to take a couple of slow, deep breaths before forcing himself to share the rest. "I came home to help my mom with the ranch because it's too much for one person to manage and there just wasn't money available to hire help. I live at home because it's cheap as well as convenient, and while my mom won't admit it, she doesn't want to be out there alone." He'd done it, managed to discuss losing his dad without irrevocably fracturing. *Point to Monroe.* "You? Do you live at home?"

7

TAYLOR KNEW SHE should've thought her question through more, but curiosity got the best of her and she'd asked. Now she had to answer in kind.

If protecting the truth is worth more than what it will cost you, lie.

The mental admonition was delivered in her father's voice and she knew, at some point, he would've said just that to her. After all, it sounded like him.

But Taylor abhorred liars. And to offer Quinn such disrespect in the face of his admission? No. She wasn't that person, wasn't her father's daughter and never had been. Not to the degree he'd expected.

"I live at home, too." She offered him a placid smile in an attempt to disguise her nerves. "I've been there a little over a year now, and I'm ready to get out. My parents and I don't get along well." She paused to bite her bottom lip and caught herself in the act, reached up to rub the action away.

Quinn gently gripped her wrist. "What are you doing?"

"I was always criticized for biting my lip when I was thinking or nervous or upset—you name it. So I try to catch myself."

His brows winged down. "Who criticized you?"

"My parents. Father said it was a giveaway that said too much when I should be saying nothing at all. Mother insisted it was neither graceful nor ladylike and should be stopped *at once*." She said the last with her mother's up-tight inflection.

Quinn's voice came so softly she had to strain to hear him. "It's actually as endearing as it is sexy, and I'd be happy to tell them so."

"I'm not sure what to…" Heat settled on her neck and cheeks. "Thank you?"

He chuckled. "My turn to ask."

She nodded, grateful to get away from the topic of why she'd ended up at home.

He met and held her gaze. "Are you involved with any-one—boyfriend, girlfriend, engaged, long-term domestic partner or anything of the sort?"

Taylor wanted to sigh at the easy question and equally easy answer. "Nope. I'm absolutely single."

"Me, too," he volunteered. "Your question."

So many things came to mind that it was hard to narrow it down to the one thing she most wanted to know. "Too many choices." Watching him, she let her mind wander and found herself asking the simplest of questions, one she wouldn't have wasted an opportunity on if she'd thought it through. "Why?"

He blinked. "Why what?"

"Never mind," she blurted. "I'll change my question."

Shaking his head, he pulled his hat off and slapped it against his thigh. "You asked, so the question stands, Tay-lor. Why what?"

"Crap." She tried to figure out how to finesse the ques-tion, but it was out there now. No undoing it or making it any better. "Okay, why are you so unarguably single?"

"Huh. Well, the easy answer is that I never found anyone I wanted to settle down with."

"I get that." A cool breeze washed over her and she lifted her face to the sky. "Um, I'm not a desert rat, but I know enough about the outdoors to know we don't want to be out here when that hits."

Quinn looked over his shoulder and cursed. "I should've been paying attention."

A thunderstorm had taken shape to the southwest, its wall cloud an ominous gray-green color with striations of lighter gray and, behind and above it, massive thunderheads. Lightning flashed cloud to cloud, but the storm was still far enough away and the lightning high enough that they didn't hear thunder. That would change. Fast.

He moved in beside her and they watched the developing storm together for a moment. Then he draped an arm over her shoulder and turned her back down the path. "We should probably start back for the horses. The forecast didn't include afternoon storms, but I'm pretty sure Noah's neighbors claimed the same thing while they sat sipping their preferred drink and made fun of the guy laboring away. C'mon."

Taylor looked around and realized that, at some point, the donkey had disappeared. "Where's our faithful companion?"

"Cob?" Quinn turned in a slow circle. "Cob!" He waited, but the animal didn't appear. "No idea. Chances are he took in the storm and headed back to the barn. He'll either catch up or, more likely, beat us home."

"Are you sure?" She worried her bottom lip with her teeth, ignoring the voice that told her to stop.

"He'll be fine. His model came with GPS."

She shrugged and held her hands up at her sides, palms skyward. "I got nothing on this one. A donkey who seems to think he's a pet and possesses a love of bottled beer, and now you're telling me he's been upgraded to include GPS."

"Best investment ever. Most of the horses have it."

"I'm sure I'm going to regret this, but what is the equivalent of equine GPS?"

"Grain Positioning Sensor. He can find his way back to his feed trough from anywhere within a thousand miles. I'll bet you—"

"Five bucks, I know. And I'm still not taking any of your bets." She kept an eye on the sky as they made their way down the steep hill.

They rounded the final corner and found Cob lounging with the horses.

Thunder began to rumble not long after they were in the saddle and Quinn had wordlessly pointed them toward the barn.

Cob moved in close to Quinn, and the cowboy kicked a foot free from the stirrup, stretching his leg out so he could rub the toe of his boot back and forth along the donkey's ribcage. The animal moved closer, forcing Quinn to adjust his seat. The cowboy grabbed the saddle horn and laughed, pushing the flat of his foot against the donkey's side. Cob bobbed his head and wagged his ears.

Quinn looked over his shoulder and caught her watching him play with the donkey. Tucking his loose foot into the stirrup, he shrugged with obviously feigned nonchalance. "What's so interesting you're compelled to stare like that?"

Heat rushed up her neck and burned across her cheeks. "Like what?"

He wheeled Jigsaw around and urged the gelding into a swift trot, riding up to her and then reining his horse in. "The hair on my neck's standing up. Then I catch you with this look on your face—a look that tells me I'm about to have to defend myself." As if he needed to emphasize his reaction, he ran a hand around the back of his neck and rubbed. "Let's just say this—if you were a predator, I wouldn't want you at my back right now. Tell me, Taylor, are you a predator hiding in plain sight?" His face relaxed a bit. "You a cougar looking for an easy meal?"

Me. A cougar. Not likely to... Wait. Easy meal? Does that mean he's willing to be a meal? Stop it, Williams. Focus. "I—I'm hardly a cougar," she sputtered. *It could mean he's flirting. But why? Oh, crap. He's smiling. He has to stop that right now.*

"By definition, you actually are. You're older than me by three months."

"Ninety days does not a cougar make." She ignored the trickle of sweat at her temple, blaming the day's heat and not the unexpected chemistry. "Besides, I haven't come on to you."

"Cougars stalk what they want, so there's rarely the need to rush. Plus the day's still young. And so am I. Impressionable to boot." He pointedly ignored her sputtering and glanced at the southwestern sky, shielding his eyes as he took in the massive storm clouds pulling together. His next words weren't directed at her but, rather, shared with her. "That's beginning to look a little more serious than I expected. We'll need to keep an eye on it as we move, but we should step it up. Weather changes out here in the blink of an eye and...hey. What's wrong? Are you okay?"

Not by anyone's definition, but thank you for asking. Honest, yes, but that wasn't what she said. Instead, she clutched the reins in one hand and wrapped her other arm around her torso. Hunching over the saddle horn, she squeezed so tight her lungs protested. "Can we please pick up the pace and get back to the barn? I don't know how to get there, and with the storm…" Panic created a wide metal band around her chest that tightened with her every breath. The sense of losing control increased until she couldn't stand it. She laid her heels to her horse's sides, the pressure gentle but insistent enough to get the gelding moving.

Hooves beat the ground and Jigsaw pulled in close to Amante, falling into step. Quinn had to raise his voice to be heard over the sound. "What? Why?"

The question was delivered with no innuendo and even less judgment. All it contained was straightforward concern. That had to be why she answered. There was no other reason she would have laid herself out there like she did.

She swallowed hard, the effort loosening the muscles in her neck and throat—muscles fear had attempted to paralyze. Then? Truth. Or…part of it. "I don't like storms. I'd prefer not to be caught out in one if I don't have to."

His brows shot up. "I've seen your qualifications, remember? You have over eight years in search and rescue—two as a grunt, four as a bona fide team member and the last two as an in-the-field rescue lead. Part of your job description has to be something like 'Must be able to thumb nose at danger and spit into the wind of an F2 tornado without getting wet.'"

When she didn't answer, he blew out a sharp, short breath and grabbed Amante's reins once again, slowing the pair of horses to a walk. "What's going on, Taylor?"

She clamped her lips together and shook her head, watching the clouds grow darker as they formed a supercell. She'd heard of this type of storm—capable of producing hail, extreme wind shear, deadly cloud-to-ground lightning, torrential rains, tornadoes. She had studied them in the classroom, since the Pacific Northwest didn't experience this particular weather phenomenon. There had been videos of storms in progress, survivor accounts, interviews with meteorologists and more. The damage these things could cause was phenomenal. Still, she'd never seen a living storm anything like this one. The way the clouds churned, it was like they were alive. Boiling. Aggressive. Growing. Hungry.

The skin along the back of her neck prickled. Smart choice was to do just as Quinn suggested and step up the pace, getting to the barn sooner rather than later. At the rate the storm was building, though, she didn't know if they'd have time to make it home before the sky unleashed its fury.

I'm not qualified to do this. I can't do this. Caution comes before courage. It has to. Survival is the ultimate win.

Clinging to the last shreds of calm she possessed, she forced herself to try to smile at Quinn. The gesture couldn't have looked better than it felt—forced, wooden, painted on. Not even Jiminy Cricket could've worked with what she had going on. "For the record, the job description lists the tornado's classification as F3."

He scowled. "Don't be cute. It's...well, it's *cute*, and that distracts me. What's going on with you?" He looked around, his scowl deepening. "The ass ran off again. I told you he was a pain. Cob!"

A rumble of thunder swallowed his shout. Amante and Jigsaw were close enough that, when the deafening sound struck, one ran into the other. Or maybe they both leaned into each other for support. Whatever the series of events, the outcome was the same. The horses collided, pushing and grinding, pinning her leg against Quinn's and tangling bits of the saddles together. She tried to pry her foot out of the stirrup, but the fender was twisted at an angle that trapped her foot.

The horses lunged forward, the saddle leather creaking under the strain of the half-ton-plus bodies pulling apart before colliding, the barrel portion of their torsos, wide from the back of the shoulder and down the ribs, grinding against each other.

Taylor couldn't stop her pained shout as stiff leather and metal buckles bruised and scraped her legs, despite the protection her jeans provided.

Quinn wrestled for control of both the horses as the two seemed to unite in purpose—achieve independence in motion at any cost.

He said something to her, a directive, given his tone. Or maybe he actually spoke to the horses. Whatever his intended outcome, it fell far short.

And then, because Life hated her—and this was proof if anyone still doubted her claim—things got worse.

The stirrup hobbles managed to twist one over the other.

Front saddle strings on each saddle wound together and create a knotted mess.

One of the Blevins buckles—his? hers?—scraped along her ankle and then fell away, clearly having come undone. There was a split second of relief as her stirrup held.

Then it fell away and chaos reigned.

Taylor had been leaning on her stirrup harder than she realized. When the support disappeared, it took her balance with it and she lurched toward Quinn.

Amante's inside rear foot came down inside the stirrup and created an anklet of the wood stirrup, pieced-out leather and broken metal bits. The whole thing flopped off the fetlock but the horse couldn't shake it no matter how hard he tried.

Quinn struggled to do whatever he thought would help.

Another boom of thunder struck on the heels of understanding, the sound so loud it must have shaken the walls and halls of heaven itself. Amante, however, seemed to be of the opinion the sound announced the appearance of the devil himself, the man in black having arrived with the single intent of riding the animal straight to hell.

The horse objected. Violently.

He arched his head as his back bowed and all four feet left the ground. Parts and pieces of the conjoined saddles snapped and flew from the epicenter of the gelding's spiritual warfare. Which, oddly, now looked more like a demonic possession in progress. The rings of white around his eyes and the froth he slung from the corners of his mouth only added to the impression.

Taylor fought to keep a leg on each side of the horse and her mind in the middle as the creature bucked and twisted, landing stiff-legged before crow hopping to the side. Seeing as she'd stuck the first and then the second landing, she imagined success might find her for once. Actively looking for the right moment to bail, she tried to adjust her foothold when she realized her bootlaces on the stirrup-less foot had become entangled in the stirrup leather and what was left of the Blevins buckle. Without shedding the shoe or cutting the laces, she couldn't get off the horse. It was no longer her choice.

Truth rang like a gong, reverberating through her entire awareness. She had no control.

Stuck.

Pinned.

Trapped.

Panic surfed the wave of bile that rushed up the back of her throat. She had to get free. Couldn't be here. Couldn't move. Couldn't see. Breath sawing in and out of her lungs, she began to fight like a mad woman, kicking and screaming and generally convincing Amante that the devil had indeed arrived.

"Slow down, Taylor," Quinn called. "Help me get Amante to calm down."

She ignored him and kept trying to work her way free.

He doesn't know. He can't know. Can't understand. No one does. No one knows what it's like to cede control and to watch people die and to survive and to hate yourself for it because you *made the call that cost them all and* you *should have been the one to diediediediedie.*

And then three things happened in rapid succession, each overlapping the other. First, lightning split the sky and the immediate crack of thunder shattered the air with a crackling boom that made her hair stand on end and her organs vibrate from the percussion.

Second, both horses took objection to the throwdown between earth and sky, particularly the resulting noise that made every mammal in the vicinity instinctively tuck tail and start looking for a place to hide. They headed different directions, breaking the last of the ties binding them together.

Amante twisted and leaped in a boneless move that saw Taylor in the saddle one moment and yanked out of her boot the next. The earth raced up, or she fell down or both. She hit with a bone-jarring *whump.*

Third, Jigsaw and Quinn reached a consensus that left Quinn in charge of the quivering animal. Man and horse spun and made their collective way to her side. Clutching the reins, Quinn dismounted and sank to his knees.

"Talk to me Taylor. Are you okay?" He pulled his smartphone from his back pocket as he surveyed her. The screen lit before he touched the display and what came out of the speaker stole the last of Taylor's control. The screeched warning, one long and then four short blasts of sound, morphed from a severe weather warning into a memory that swallowed Taylor whole.

THE CHOPPER PITCHED and then plummeted, catapulting her stomach into her throat. Bile welded it in place. Warnings *flashed on the instrument panel's digital displays. Dials spun wildly. A sharp, screeching alarm registered in layers, coming through the speakers on her headset before weaseling its way between her skin and the headset's ear cushions. The wind screamed like a wounded animal and shoved the chopper sideways, indiscriminately rattling bolts and teeth alike. A man cursed. Static overrode the tirade with a menacing hiss.*

A male voice shouted and was answered in kind.

Harsh words were exchanged, words fueled not by anger but by undiluted fear. And yet none of it mattered.

Glass shattered.

Metal groaned and then screamed under force it was never meant to bear.

Chaos reigned, and there would be no independence from its tyranny.

If hell had a soundtrack, it probably sounded a lot like this.

8

QUINN GRIPPED JIGSAW'S reins in one hand and shoved the SAT phone into his back pocket with the other. He had to trust that the horse would sort himself out and stand still like he'd been trained to do.

Because that worked out so well with Amante.

Worrying over that would have to wait until later. Right now, he had to get to Taylor.

He couldn't have had a better view of the impromptu rodeo she'd inadvertently starred in if he'd bought the best seats in the house. She'd landed hard and then curled in on herself, wrapping one arm around her middle and the other over her head. Then she'd gone almost preternaturally still.

Kneeling beside her, he reached out to touch her and stopped inches short of her bare upper arms. There was a field assessment protocol to follow for his safety and hers. The problem? His mind was fixated on her in a way that made everything secondary. Even common sense and especially rational thought.

Visual assessment first.

Man, he hated forced sensibleness—hated more that sensibleness had to be forced. Particularly on him.

Dropping to his knees beside her, he took her in with

a rapid glance. She'd lost a boot in the course of things. If there were such a thing as "professional dusting," her jeans would be the height of fashion. The tank top she wore had a tear on the front hem. Her braided hair had hung in there, but it was still more flyaway than he'd ever seen. A rapidly coloring deep bruise on her arm would end up dark purple within the hour and would slow her down some, particularly in her climb re-cert. Something about the impending climb was bothering him, though, and he'd been at this game long enough to have developed a healthy respect for intuition. Even superstition.

All of that could be dealt with later. Right now, he needed to get her back to the ranch and, possibly, into town to see the doctor. Or, worse, into the city to the hospital.

Taylor's unmoving form was unnaturally pale against the living blanket of grass where she lay. Panic took a vicious swipe at him, raking its claws down his psyche and leaving deep runnels that fear rushed to fill. If something was horribly wrong, he didn't have access to immediate medical care. Hell, there was no one to call for help. He'd been gone so long that, with his mom out of town, he didn't know who among old friends or current neighbors would answer if he did. He was balls deep and sinking slowly. It would be nice if, just once, Fate would throw him a rope. Truth? That bitch was more likely to toss him an anchor just to watch him sink faster. If Taylor was going to get out of this mess, he would be the one to make it happen. Alone.

Is this what happened with Dad? No, because he was alone. If I'd been here, I would have been with him. I should *have been with him. I could have stopped this whole thing from happening.* His eyes burned. *God, please don't let him have suffered.*

Shaking almost uncontrollably, he threw protocol aside and reached out. He had to touch her. Period. Her bare arm was nearest him, so he traced a finger down her biceps. She twitched—more a hard shiver, really—and something in him settled. He could do this, get them back to the house. It had been fear, not rationality, prodding him seconds before. His instinct was to shut everything, and everyone, down, to create silence and put things in order. To save her from the fear that rode her hard. If he could establish order, he could—and would—command control, and he needed control. Now.

"Taylor?" he called, his voice diminished, forced to compete with all the other noise. Still on his knees, he shuffled a little closer.

She neither moved nor responded.

Reaching out, he laid one hand flat against her upper chest. The heel settled above her cleavage while his fingers rested against the base of her throat. It wasn't a touch meant to arouse but to create a connection.

Taylor jerked upright like a marionette whose strings had been yanked taut by uncoordinated hands. Her eyes shot open, wide and devoid of anything but terror. She grabbed his forearms with a little mewling sound, digging her fingernails deep enough into his skin that he winced.

His phone vibrated against his butt. Had she not held his arms, he would have grabbed the phone and shut it down, but he didn't want to break her hold on him. Three quick jolts—*bzz-bzz-bzz*—followed, a precursor to the incoming severe weather warning. Then came the unmistakable alarm. The obnoxious noise ripped across the air, assaulting his hearing just as the storm's first large, cold raindrops pelted his skin.

Taylor's response to—either? both?—was instantaneous and not at all anticipated.

She went rigid, her face blank, eyes losing any hint of emotion, personality or awareness. Sweat beaded along her brow, collecting and then breaking to trickle down her near temple. Beneath his hand, her heart beat against her chest as if it was desperate to break out, get away, escape the madness that its physical host refused to flee.

"No!" And then she screamed, her shrill cry joining the cacophony around him.

Quinn didn't think. Or, if he did, it wasn't with his frontal lobe. Instinct drove him to react, to protect. And he did.

Reaching for her at the same time she leaped for him, they crashed together and toppled to the ground. He twisted to take the brunt of the fall. Taylor didn't give him time to recover, instead scrambling up the front of his body and wrapping her arms around his neck and her legs around his waist. She clung to him with the force of newly paired, industrial-strength Velcro pressed together by a ten-ton steamroller. Could skin-to-skin contact that occurred under extreme force result in a cold weld? Probably. Because he was pretty damn sure it was going to take a vat of Crisco, basting brushes, the Jaws of Life and a priest to pry them apart.

Fine by him. It meant they'd be here awhile.

He held her tight, one arm cradling her butt while he cupped her head with his free hand. His fingers moved of their own volition, petting and stroking and massaging her until she shuddered and sighed.

She buried her face against his neck and breathed deep, mumbling something into his skin.

Not a word of what she said made any sense, but that wasn't what struck Quinn in the very center of who he was. What leveled him was his overwhelming need to protect the woman in his arms. To see her safe. To chase her personal demons from the dark corners of her mind. And he was likely the least-qualified man in the county to see that through.

Didn't change the fact he wanted it, though.

So, what kind of history did this woman have?

Lightning struck close by, and Jigsaw began pawing the ground, agitation rolling off him in waves.

"Hang tight, buddy, and I'll get us home."

Quinn didn't promise when that might happen or the condition they'd be in when they arrived. He could offer optimism but couldn't stomach a liar.

Tucking his chin, he tried to get a look at Taylor, but her face was hidden against his neck and she didn't seem inclined to move. She still trembled, though, and her skin was chilled despite the unseasonable afternoon heat the storm had pushed toward them. Those physical aftershocks were smaller than the main event had been, but were still, at times, hard enough to clack her teeth together. In his opinion, the shadows and memories that ate at Taylor looked a hell of a lot like post-traumatic stress.

Quinn wasn't under the delusion he was qualified to issue a diagnosis like that. He was a cowboy, not a psychologist.

What Quinn *was*, however, was observant. The result? He'd watched people long enough to learn a lot about them. For years he'd seen climbers show up too determined to conquer a climb. Some folks came clearheaded and ready to face the challenges required to summit. Others would show up and, despite their best efforts, it quickly became clear that what they needed to conquer wasn't a mountain but a memory.

Each had a different story about how they'd ended up in front of him. Some had gone up the mountain and, along the way, found a good place to lay their excess burden down. They would come off the mountain rejuvenated, different, *renewed*. Others couldn't bear to part with their trauma or grief. Sometimes they'd try, sometimes they wouldn't. The end result was the same. They'd make it back to base camp unchanged by the experience and would go back to their lives as burdened as they'd been when he met them.

He had no idea which camp Taylor fell into, but it concerned him. A lot. If he took her up and she froze, she could become a liability. A life-or-death liability. He wasn't ready for that.

How did she end up in this condition?

The answer was as relevant as it was irrelevant. Bottom line, he had to know she could make the climb without putting him, or search and rescue if they had to be called out, at risk. If he couldn't be sure she would perform at two-thousand-plus feet, he had to stop the climb.

His stomach clenched so hard he fought the urge to double over and curl into himself. Calling stop on the climb brought him right back to the original issue—returning her money. But to keep on with the climb was to potentially assign a dollar figure to the lives he could be putting in jeopardy, including his own. If things were bad now, what would happen to his mom if he died? Or, oddly worse, if he were seriously injured and had to have medical care? He didn't have the kind of insurance that would help much. Why?

He gritted his teeth at the answer.

He couldn't afford it.

Everything seemed to come back to money and the fact there was never enough.

Lightning flashed. The resulting thunder cracked and rumbled immediately, forcing Quinn to stop waxing philosophical and get his head in the game. Training kicked in and ushered emotion into the wings.

No matter what skills Taylor listed on her résumé, that was paper. This was life. If she couldn't access those skills and help him problem-solve while fear ruled her, she couldn't help. That meant the challenge of getting them out of this rested on his shoulders.

Fishing blindly around the ground behind him, he brushed the felt rim of his cowboy hat with his fingers. He twisted and scooted and pushed with his heels until he managed to retrieve the black Stetson and get it situated. It took a couple of tries and some creative language to successfully lumber to his feet with Taylor still barnacled to his front.

Okay. First things first. What do I have to work with?

He glanced at their immediate surroundings before making a short circuit around the area where Amante had gone rodeo star and came to a stop a few feet from Jigsaw. "You, my man, are the only tool out here. The only solution I need. Am I right?"

Jigsaw let his eyes close as he hung his head, his ears flagging as he cocked one hip. The tip of the corresponding hoof skimmed the ground.

"Nice try, won't fly. You're no killdeer, so stand up and stop flapping your version of a broken wing."

Horse.

That was it.

"Son of a bitch," he muttered, trying to shift Taylor so that his center of gravity *was* center.

Had he not been so caught up in analyzing his next steps and making a focused effort to pay attention to the woman in his arms, the condition of his surroundings would have registered. As it was, the atmospheric change didn't strike him as odd or even "other." Not until everything went eerily still.

Quinn's entire body went taut, and he pulled Taylor closer to his chest. The storm's weight was enormous. He hadn't experienced anything like this in years. Time away from the Southwest's high plains had softened instincts his dad had carefully cultivated over the first twenty years of his life. Those instincts were the ones that kept a man alive when the threat came, not with voice or fist, but in scent and scene.

Clouds, colored like an aged bruise, closed in and towered over him, and the sharp scent of rain on dry desert air permeated every cell in his body. The storm's energy pulsed against his skin like an external heartbeat. Soft wind dropped off, pulled back and gathered itself, preparing to unleash an assault that had the potential to destroy in moments what it had taken lifetimes to build. Dirt devils swirled, small at first, and then gathering speed. They spun higher, faster, picking up anything within reach that could be weaponized before it was thrown. Sand became sandpaper against the skin. Small twigs and mesquite branches were wielded like tiny shivs.

And there Quinn stood, exposed.

Man, he knew better than this—knew better than to let the storm gain enough momentum that outrunning it was no longer an option. He had to get them someplace that offered at least basic shelter. He looked around again, was lost in thought, when it hit him.

Granite Mantel.

The place was a simple granite overhang, about forty feet wide and sixty feet deep. It had become a popular place for settlers to stop for a day or two, parking their wagons at the front of the overhang and camping deeper in. There were even a few Native American petroglyphs on the walls. Not only would it be an easy place to shelter, but it was on the way home. When everything blew over, they'd head back and, when he was sure she was only bruised but not broken, he'd insist she come clean on what had pushed her over the edge out here.

Decision made, he started toward Jigsaw.

Thunder rumbled, and Quinn stroked Taylor's back as her trembling intensified. He shifted his hold on her, catching a quick glimpse of wide eyes as he did. Encouraged that she'd at least lifted her head, he tried to draw her farther out of the place she'd mentally fled to. "You know, you're better than those old motel beds you'd put a quarter into so they'd vibrate."

She either cursed him blue or laughed, her warm breath heating the skin of his neck. He wanted to believe she had laughed. Until she told him otherwise, he was going to go with that as the easy answer.

9

TAYLOR WAS SOAKED THROUGH, deeply bruised and worn out. Hell of a combination.

With one shoe on and one shoe likely still attached to Amante's saddle, she crouched down in a butt-to-heel-and-knees-to-chest position. She was freezing. Wrapping her arms around her shins, she held tight in an attempt to stave off the shivers while she waited for her internal body temperature to come home to roost. The brilliant orange flames of the campfire Quinn had started offered rudimentary warmth since her clothes were wet, but she wasn't complaining. The man had made fire with two pieces of flint and some twine from his saddlebag.

Seriously. Quinn was some kind of Discovery Channel yet-to-be-discovered superhero who would probably eat bugs while discussing their nutritional value. Starting a fire was nothing for a man like that.

Rain had plastered his shirt to his torso and his jeans to his thighs. Mysteriously, his hat was in nearly perfect shape, despite having been tossed around, stomped on and generally abused. They'd been riding Jigsaw in tandem when she'd asked how he'd managed to preserve his hat.

He'd solemnly replied, "Cowboy trade secret."

She'd laughed and, without thinking, leaned against his chest, shivering when he'd settled his hands at her waist.

Not once had he brought up her little episode. And now, with each second that passed without comment, this conversational elephant added both height and breadth to its mass. The invisible animal currently had his hip in her face and had forced her back to the wall.

She didn't like the way Quinn moved around quietly, casting her sidelong looks but not speaking to her. It made her anxious and irritable. Or more anxious and more irritable. It wasn't as if she'd started out at center on that particular field.

The knowledge that Quinn could drop the conversational boom on her at any moment, asking her questions she didn't want to answer, had her fidgeting even as she tried to shrink into the shadows.

"How many more times are you going to look at me like I'm about to make a rude noise with my lip followed by a cryptic reference to fava beans?"

His deep voice filled the space without warning, and she nearly came out of her skin.

"Considering you just stopped my heart in my chest, probably only once or twice. Then you're scot-free." She hated how breathy she sounded, all Marilyn Monroe does happy birthday. If someone had to *sound* like that, they should have the benefit of *looking* like that.

"You saying you need mouth-to-mouth?" His lips curled up at one corner. "Because I'd volunteer for that duty."

"Funny guy." Still, heat stung her cheeks.

"Only when I'm joking." He stopped what he was doing—running a small cloth over Jigsaw's coat—and came over to sit by her.

She started when he casually touched her arm.

He didn't comment, just kept rubbing his hand up and

down her arm. The way she'd been balled up like a little armadillo hadn't given her the chance to create space between them, and he took advantage of the fact, pulling her in close to his side. Heavily muscled arms came around her and shifted her onto his lap, legs folded tailor style. Leaning against the rock wall, he closed his eyes…but didn't relax his grip. "You need to slow down, Taylor. We're here for a while, so make the most of it."

"Make the most of…" She snorted, the derisive sound swallowed by the space before it reached the stone ceiling. When she attempted to twist around to face him, he clamped his arms around her but didn't succeed in keeping her from catching everything that passed over his face. *Pain. Hunger. Consequence.* Anything else was lost when he yanked his hat off, dropped it beside them and began bouncing his head against the cave wall over and over.

She twisted toward him with obvious purpose, and this time he didn't balk. Instead, he let her face him.

"Hey," she said quietly, not attempting to hide her concern. "No damaging the guide. It's a rule."

"I don't remember that line in my contract." He might have argued. But he didn't. Instead, he stopped and let his head rest against the rough stone.

"Invisible ink. You totally should have checked me on that, considering all you agreed to."

A tired smile drifted over his face. "Like?"

"Oh, you know. Little things." At his arched brow and amused look, she lifted her chin and met his stare head-on. "If your truck is nicer than mine, it's mine. If I like your gear better than mine, it's mine. If you have a dog I bond with and he—or she—gets in my new truck that used to be yours, the animal is mine. If—"

He pulled her against his chest and held her tight, his

lips pressed against the crown of her head. "I think I get the picture."

The affectionate gesture confused her so much she didn't struggle but rather sat, quiet and contemplative, in Quinn's lap. An image of him on stage in a mish-mash of costumes—cowboy hat, safety helmet, headlamp, crampons strapped to cowboy boots, rope for each persona, D-rings, a pistol strapped to his side—made her giggle.

"What's that about?" he asked with mock demand.

"You on stage, all oiled up, shirt being shredded by your rabid fans as you bump and grind to something by Toby Keith." She was giggling at that point, foolish as it was.

"You're imagining me as a *stripper*?" he asked, his voice a bit high. "Good grief, woman. I'm trying to decide the best way to open a conversation and here you are mentally stripping me down to…to… What do male strippers wear?"

"Thongs with ridiculous spangly crap over the junk." She hiccupped with her laughter. "Yours would be a sheriff's star, of course."

He tipped her chin up and her heart stuttered. That smile was back. "Speculation, or are you speaking from experience?"

"Speculation, of course."

"Well, in the interest of good sportsmanship and my own need to represent my people well, I'm going to suggest you add assless chaps to my routine." He waggled brows. "And a stick horse named Rex."

Taylor's breath hitched. She felt her eyes go impossibly wide. Her fingers curled into the material of his shirt. And she tipped over the edge. Laughter erupted from her in peals she was helpless to stop. It went on until her ribs ached for reasons other than her high-impact introduction to the ground. She lifted her face to his, laughter still riding her words. "Stick horse." The look on his face had her croaking out a single word. "What?"

He reached up and cradled her jaw with one hand. "You're beautiful when you laugh."

Beautiful.

How had they gone from hostility to a trail ride to an elephant between them to this, whatever it was? How? It couldn't happen for her. *Shouldn't* happen for her. And she knew it. Quinn's words didn't mean anything. They couldn't. He didn't know what she was responsible for, didn't realize that, just an hour before, she'd begun to remember what had happened. What if, when he found out, he didn't want anything to do with her? He had a right to make that choice. Damn if it didn't hurt, though, and that surprised her. That it would matter what he thought.

She turned her chin away from his hand. "You're wonderful to say so, but you can't mean it, Quinn. Not the way a woman wants a man to mean it. You can't," she insisted when his brow creased and he opened his mouth, presumably to argue. "You don't know me."

"No jokes, Taylor. No dodging whatever's happening here. No bullshit." He ran his hand up her back, reached the tie on her braid and undid it. With slow precision, he began to undo her hair. "And for the record, I mean it exactly the way a man means it when he finally figures out what that off-balance feeling is when he's around a woman he's attracted to."

"Off-balance feeling?" she parroted through numb lips.

"Pretty much, yeah. It's like the world tilts when he's not with her. It's like nothing works quite right." He moved then, seeming to lift and twist and stretch all at once. "Then she shows up and everything is somehow right in ways it hadn't been even seconds before."

Taylor squeezed her eyes closed. "Don't complicate this, Quinn."

"Too late."

His lips whispered over hers, a request unspoken in the tender touch—a chance for her to turn him away before they took the next step. But she didn't. Wouldn't. Couldn't. For the first time since she'd come to after the accident, the vast emptiness in her chest yielded to the warmth of hope. And she wanted that more than anything.

Taylor wanted a single chance to hope for what might be, in the face of what was.

QUINN SHIFTED SO Taylor was beneath him, his chest pressed to hers just tight enough that he could feel the rapid rise and fall of her breath and the machine-gun rhythm of her heart. He could relate.

Dragging his palm from her chin, down her throat, over her breastbone and between her breasts had to be similar to a junkie's first hit of the prime stuff. She was rich and lush, firmly muscled yet plush, planed smooth by hard work yet possessing dips and valleys that declared her all woman. Every bit of her came together to create a body made for carnal worship.

He smiled against her mouth.

Never thought I'd be the religious type.

She nipped his bottom lip, demanding his full attention.

Quinn was happy to not only oblige but atone for the sin of letting his mind wander for even a moment.

When he pushed up to rest on one forearm, her dexterous fingers went to his jeans and plucked the hem of his T-shirt from the confines of his waistband. Cold fingertips brushed over his lower abdomen and he sucked in a sharp breath, his back bowing. The response was involuntary.

She made the most of the revealed skin, dragging her

short, blunt nails up his six-pack. Her hands had been calloused once. The heavier skin felt different, more substantial, against his chest, while the pads of her fingers were smooth.

A small sound, hungry and almost feral, scraped its way up the back of his throat when she hooked one leg around his waist and ground her mons against the length of his erection. The move was aggressive, and he responded in kind. Dominating her mouth thrilled him. Their tongues thrust against each other and then stroked with surprise tenderness, every touch and caress suggestive of two bodies loving each other wholly and completely. As much as he wanted to bury himself in her and lose himself to the deep, instinctive rhythm, he needed the kiss more. And so did she. He'd gladly give her both, want and need. They had time.

When she nipped his bottom lip hard enough it stung, he wanted to praise her. When she laved that little wound and sucked it gently between her lips, he wanted to fall at her feet and worship her. The total dichotomy of this woman had set him spinning like a top from their first meeting. He was dizzy in her.

He wasn't sure he ever wanted to be steady on his feet again.

Drunk on the taste of her—smooth caramel and crisp apple—and drowning in her scent—sunshine and fir—he was thoroughly debauched.

Taylor whimpered as she tugged at his shirt. "Off."

He swallowed the word before fulfilling the request.

Quinn leaned over her and then into her, hiking her leg up and hooking her knee around his hip. She adjusted her position so she cradled his sex with hers. They fit together as if they'd been designed for this very thing. The heat pulsing between them was a raw ache only consummation would resolve. Nothing had ever felt so right. The thought should have scared him, but it didn't.

Pushing up on his elbow gave her room to caress his chest, and she did. Her touches grew bold, even possessive. When she pinched his nipple and followed by breaking the kiss to dart low and stroke the sensitive skin with the tip of her tongue, he couldn't contain his shouted encouragement. The way she incorporated lips and teeth and tongue was a departure from his past experience. Hell's denizens would host an ice cream social before he went back to what had once satisfied him.

Quinn gripped Taylor's hips and executed a swift roll, situating her atop his groin. He arched up into her as he pulled her against him; she took the initiative to rock. Her hair was loose and wild, a halo of dark curls he wanted draped on either side of his face, a curtain they could hide behind that would narrow the world down to just the two of them. Then thoughts scattered to the four corners when she began to ride him with wanton abandon, arching her back and pushing her hands through her hair.

He bucked hard at the sight.

Her feminine sound of encouragement was saturated with pleasure.

So he did it again.

Taylor gasped and fell forward, parking her hands on the pads of muscle on his chest.

Thunder rumbled in the distance, the sound of the rain like a locomotive barreling down the tracks, its engine wide open.

Time took on a different value, slowing to allow him to pick up the fine details of her body as she slowly lowered her chin. The demand in her gaze bored into him and he swore he heard something like the starting gun in a hundred-yard sprint. The problem? Quinn was hungry for her. Starving. There was no way to slow things down and make this an endurance event. Hell, they'd be lucky if what happened between them didn't set new speed records, when all was said and done.

He was going to embarrass himself, but he'd make it up to her.

Reclaiming her mouth, he took the kiss deep, bathing in their mutual desire. Then he reached for her shirt.

His fingers traced over a hard, high ridge of skin, and he froze.

A sound of sheer distress escaped Taylor before she scrambled off his lap.

"Taylor?" He sat up, his world spinning. "Baby, what's wrong? What is it?"

Her face was so pale, her skin approached translucent in the firelight.

Rolling to his knees, he adjusted his eager erection behind the unforgiving denim. The thing needed obedience classes. Plural. "Talk to me, Taylor."

"It's a scar," she whispered.

That wasn't what he meant. He started to clarify, to explain that he didn't care about physical scars. What worried him was her well-being. Nothing more. But when he looked at her, searching her face, he found in the depths of her eyes a bitterness he'd never witnessed. "I don't care about scars, honey."

"You'll care about this one."

His brows drew together of their own volition. "Why?"

"Because I got it the day I killed seven men."

He sank down, resting his butt against his boot heels, his erection deflating faster than an air mattress on a honeymoon camping trip.

I'll take A Kick to the Balls for three hundred, Alex.

10

A PERVASIVE CHILL spread through Taylor and left her far colder than before. Why in the world had she blurted that out? Panic? It had to be. Because there was killing the mood and then there was what she'd just done—slitting its proverbial throat and picking up the phone to casually make funeral plans while she watched her victim bleed out at her feet.

She gestured with her hands, trying to substitute actions for what really required words to satisfy. Finally she gave up and sank to the ground across from the man who didn't deserve to be dragged through her nightmare. Not any of it.

"So." He gave her a strange look. "Seven men, huh?"

She nodded.

Quinn's throat worked, his fingers digging into his denim-clad thighs. "Care to explain? Because my head has gone to a very weird place where my story ends up being made into a Lifetime movie, but not until I've had a solid run on the legal review channel where the actor chosen to play me isn't really a good fit." He paused and blew out a breath. "If I'm going to end up a cold case, let's get it over with."

"It isn't something to joke about." There was an undercurrent of anger rising in her despite her voice's flat tone and her soul's raw ache.

"Oddly, I'm not joking." Stretching his fingers wide, he settled his palms on his thighs. "Where did the scars come from, Taylor? How did the men die?"

This was the conversation she'd dreaded. She didn't deserve his compassion and yet hadn't earned his fear. Divided, she worried her bottom lip with her teeth.

"You throw something like that out there, you better be ready to nut up and own it," Quinn said, the censure in his voice as clear as a gin spring.

"You want to know?" she bit out and then laughed, the sound coarse, even caustic. "So do I. There's nothing I wouldn't give to be able to remember, Quinn. I was the one who made the decisions that sent them to their deaths. I need to know what happened. You know what?" She lurched to her feet and took several jerky steps toward the wide mouth of their shelter. "I want to leave. Now. When I get back to the cottage, I'll pack my stuff and get out of your hair."

"Just like that."

She lifted her chin. Defiance wasn't a good look for her, but she'd gravitate toward it when her choice was that or self-pity. Yep. Defiance won every time the two squared off.

"I see." Quinn's face went blank and his eyes followed suit, locking away anything and everything he might have been thinking. "And your recertification?"

"I'm calling it off," she finished for him. "Keep the money. I don't need it, don't want it back." She would go back to her parents' place in Virginia, take a few days to get herself together. Then she'd reach out to an instructor in Wyoming. He offered the same classes, but they didn't have as much prep work. If she could hold out, keep the panic attacks at bay until she was up the mountain, she could make it work. And if she couldn't?

Mind-numbing emptiness stopped the direction her thoughts were headed. Failing to recertify simply couldn't happen.

"How are the scars and your running related?"

She spun around and her nose ended up nearly parked on his chest. Craning her neck, she scowled up at him. "None of your business."

"The hell it isn't! If you think I'm about to take you up the mountain and put our lives in jeopardy for you to get your re-cert, you're selling yourself a boxful of nothing at a premium price. You want to go up? Talk to me." He turned his back to her, his chin dipping to his chest. "Don't do this to me."

"Excuse me?" she spat. "This isn't about you."

He spun around and took a fractional step forward. "In case no one else has had the cojones to tell you, self-righteous indignation doesn't pair well with the whole girl-next-door thing you're working." They were close enough that when he crossed his arms over his chest, his forearms brushed her chest. "That one? Yeah, I bought into it once. Don't count on my repeat business."

She sucked in a sharp breath and took a clumsy step away. "I was never for sale, you jackass."

"And I don't buy my companionship," he retorted. "What the hell happened to you, Taylor?" He stepped closer and his entire demeanor changed, softened. "I'm not asking to be nosy or to compromise your privacy or exploit you in any way. I need to know."

Memories rushed her, a jumble of overlapping events she needed to sort out. Time had reduced to whispers those voices she'd once been able to remember. Faces were blurred, no more than watery images with little definition.

The five men she'd partnered with in search and rescue deserved more than her continued avoidance. They were due their place, their sacrifice acknowledged, the lives they'd lived remembered. No one could do that for them the way she could.

"Bad memories are unique in that the farther you run, the more stamina they develop. The more you fear them, the more power they wield. They evolve into emotional terrorists who know exactly where to hit you to hurt you the most. They will chase you as long as you keep running. I know. I've been running a long time and have the emotional wounds as proof."

She pressed trembling fingers to her lips. "When does it stop?"

He curled a finger under her chin, lifting her face to his. "It stops when you decide it stops. When you say enough is enough and you face it head-on."

"I'm not that person." All the psychologists, psychiatrists, other medical doctors—not one had helped her reach that point.

Quinn caught her chin between his forefinger and thumb and held it tight. "Look at me."

The first tear rolled over her bottom lashes.

"Look at me," the man in front of her growled.

She forced herself to do as told. His strength fueled her strength, which, in turn, choked out her weakness. The two were mutually exclusive and could not occupy the same space.

His smile was almost nonexistent. Almost, but not quite, not when the deep emotion in his gaze was so warm. "That's my girl."

He leaned in until she could see only his darkened eyes, smell only the sun and rain that coated his skin, hear each breath, recall the decadent taste of his lips and the feel of his strong hands on her.

"Keep looking at me like that and I'll forget the rest of what I want to say."

"Say it fast."

Wrapping a hand around the back of her neck, he gave her a solemn nod. "You say you're not that person? You're wrong, Taylor. *Wrong*." He squeezed. "Do you hear me?"

"I don't know how to do this." The admission tore something inside her and her knees threatened to buckle.

He simply tightened his hold on her. "You do what you have to do. You take one step at a time and you face forward. Don't look back."

"But—"

Forehead to forehead now, his gaze drilled into her. "Don't. Look. Back. You're not going that way. Your life is in front of you."

She had a brief moment to wonder what it meant that he was the most immediate thing in front of her, and then he shattered the fragile barrier his words had built between her and the past.

"Tell me what happened."

QUINN HAD A niggling suspicion that this confessional conversation would dredge up so many skeletons they could start a haunted house or lease the lot out for Halloween parties. Sure, he could direct the conversation. Encouraging her to face down the very things that had chased her into his embrace in the first place would be easy enough. But that wouldn't be fair. In order to gain her trust in this, he'd have to practice a little give and take. It sucked when his words came back to bite him in the back pocket.

Coaxing her forward, he sat down near where they'd been before, when… He chanced a heavy-lidded glance at her and found she'd beaten him to The Look. She considered him with expressive, hungry eyes. The heart, and heat, of her gaze played out when he gestured for her to take a seat.

She looked around. "You really think this is the best venue?"

"C'mon, Taylor. It's not like we have anywhere to be or the means to get there if we did."

Shrugging in a disjointed way, she sank to the floor. "Quid pro quo."

"Huh?"

She smiled a bit absently. "Your idea, actually. You mentioned fava beans earlier and got me thinking. If you want something from me, you'll give me something in return."

"What do you want?"

"Now who's skeptical?" she teased before gesturing. "You want me to lay myself bare? Then you'll do the same. Go on. You first."

"Nope. Given your preseduction admission, you're up." He leaned back on one hand and locked his elbow. "But I'll make you a deal."

"You've progressed from betting to dealing. Evolution in motion."

"Smartass." Stretching a leg out, he toed her with his boot. "Let's up the stakes a little bit."

"Aaaand, back to betting. Darwin would have had a field day with you."

He fought off a smile, equally amused and irritated she could coax laughter from him when there wasn't much to laugh about. "I'm going to ask you a question. If you don't answer thoroughly, you shed a piece of clothing."

If a spine could snap straight, hers would have cracked the air like a bullwhip. "Strip interrogation? I don't think so."

The most important thing was that she believe he had control of the situation. Otherwise, she'd balk and lock down. If maintaining the facade of control meant he had to push her, he would. People were looser with their words when they were rattled. "I'm going to see that scar, Taylor. It's a matter of when, not if."

"You presumptuous bastard."

Bingo. Frazzled.

Wrapping her arms around her middle, she glared at him. "Go on, then. What do you want to know?"

"How did you get the scar?"

"I don't remember."

"Give me your shoe."

"I only have one," she protested.

He just held out his hand, palm up, and wiggled his fingers.

"No." She stood, far more graceful than she'd been earlier, and began to pace. "You don't get to make me 'lose' where this is concerned." Her voice constricted until her words sounded as if they were squeezed between two sides of an iron vice. "I keep my clothes."

Slow and controlled, Quinn shifted to sitting upright and dipped his chin in a short, sharp nod. "Then tell me what happened."

Beginning with very little history, she jumped to the morning that had changed her life. In short sentences, simple language and crisply articulated words, she explained that she'd been the captain of an elite search and rescue team. Her team had been made up of her plus five men, and they were tight. They'd worked together as an exclusive SAR team for almost seven years, and their recovery rate was phenomenal. She referenced several rescues in Mount Rainier National Park, but that didn't make sense. The address on all her paperwork listed Rising Rock, Virginia, as her mailing address. Just like that, the nagging sense of awareness that had been dogging him was back and stronger than ever.

She couldn't live in the Northeast and work in the Pacific Northwest, yet she'd asserted both were true.

He was noodling over the references to the Pacific Northwest in general when she made mention of the fact that Washington's weather was volatile. He held up a hand, palm out in a stop-motion gesture. "Hold on. You're from Virginia."

Her brows drew together and little furrows marred her forehead. "Yes."

"If you're from tobacco country, what are you doing working in the land of fine wine and Sasquatch sightings?" He dragged a hand over his face and took a quick glance outside. *Excellent. It's stopped raining. We'll be able to head home soon.* The word Rainier registered in his foggy brain and the world narrowed and his vision followed suit. "Say that again."

"What? What part?" she asked, obviously confused.

"Rainier." He closed his eyes and focused on the sound of her voice, low and melodic, and the accompanying sound of his heartbeat. They sounded good together.

Understanding clicked into place like tumblers in an industrial lock—a succession of rapid, loud, heavy clicks that followed one right after the other.

"Quinn?"

Taylor. The white noise became deafening, and he couldn't shake it. He needed it to go away so he could *think*. He needed to get out of here and look up the information he'd seen on the climb that had cost seven men— five search and rescue, the helo pilot and one climber in peril—their lives. How could she be the captain who'd made the call? *Taylor.* The news had reported the captain had been a man. *Taylor.* Or had, in fact, failed to report that *she* wasn't male. A little hitch in his chest made him gasp. *Hadn't the captain been medivaced to a level one trauma center?* His hand went to his abs and spread wide, mimicking the place he'd felt the scar. *Hadn't he been grievously injured?* He hadn't put the two individual ideas together because the woman in front of him was from freaking *Virginia.* And he knew she wasn't a man. "Why didn't you tell me who you are?"

A rapid flash of confusion colored her face in a variety of pink hues. Then her half smile fell away and took all semblance of color with it. The color that had made her look so alive was replaced with a gray pallor not often seen on the living. Her throat worked as she tried to swallow. At his continued silence, her chin went up and her eyes darkened. There were memories there. Memories he wouldn't want for any amount of money. "Would it have made a difference in whether or not you agreed to take me up?"

He wouldn't lie to her and didn't know what to say beyond, "I don't know."

"Then there's your answer." The magnitude of sorrow made the air thick. "So, how much do you know?"

"Only what I've read."

"You and the rest of the world," she said, so quietly he strained to hear her. Shivering, she closed in on what was left of the fire, palms held out to the embers. "If you've read the reports then you know as much as I do."

"You're telling me you don't remember anything about that day." He couldn't disguise the skepticism that rose to the surface.

Muscles at the back of her jaw moved, giving away the fact she'd gritted her teeth. It took her a minute to get herself together and answer. "You don't think I want to remember?"

"Why would you?"

Jerking around, she moved too quickly and lost her balance, her nonbooted foot tangling with her laces and sending her sprawling. She landed on her hands and knees. Hazel eyes glinted at him through that waterfall of hair, but this wasn't going down anywhere near the way he'd imagined it.

"Why *would* I want to remember?" she spat, rising to her knees and shoving at strands of hair that caught at the corner of her mouth. "Those men are owed justice, Quinn. If I made the call that killed them, I need to know."

"And how does your knowing bring them justice?" he pressed, truly trying to understand.

But that, that last question, may have taken everything too far.

Absolute anguish created fissures in her, visible in her slightly parted lips, the frown lines beside her mouth, the tiny crow's feet that formed as her eyes narrowed, the way the tendons in her neck stood out just enough to cast a shallow shadow. There were undoubtedly more, but he couldn't look away from her face. As fast as the fissures appeared, they were gone, ghosting away so he wondered if he'd seen them at all. But, again, her eyes told the story her face tried to hide. They bled with so many dense emotions he couldn't breathe. How the hell did she manage to put one foot in front of the other every day, let alone carve out a life in the aftermath?

Slowly rising to her feet, she bent to untie her one boot and toe it off. Head bent, she managed to hide from him in the small space. "I'm done here, Quinn. Help me get back to the cottage. It won't take me long to pack. If you don't mind, I'd like to stay one more night so I can start out tomorrow fresh."

"Start out tomorrow." The words were as thick as raw honey on his tongue.

"I'm done. I'm obviously not going to be able to recertify." She held up a hand to stop his intended rebuttal. "No, Quinn. I'm done. I should never have sought you out, never petitioned you to see me through the course and field work. I'll get back to Washington, wrap things up and…" Her chest rose and fell in erratic, jerky movements. "We'll see. One step at a time, I suppose."

And just where did that leave him?

I'll take Out in the Cold for $100, Alex.

11

THE BARN CAME into view shortly after dark. Taylor didn't even make it all the way there, sliding off Jigsaw's back without comment and leaving horse and rider in her wake as she made her way toward the cabin. It wasn't entirely, or remotely, fair to leave Quinn to handle the two horses and Cob—the two runaways having been waiting at the barn as if nothing had happened. The problem was, she couldn't manage to keep herself vertical.

Tall grass and wildflowers whispered as she passed, tapping her knees as she crossed the field. She wished they'd made it just an hour earlier so she wouldn't have to go into the dark cabin alone. There was no help for it, though.

By the time she reached the cottage, she was running on yesterday's fumes. That didn't stop her from letting out a small, "Woo-hoo." And when she started up the steps with feet that felt cast in lead, each one she conquered felt like a skirmish won in the battle to reach her bed. She wouldn't claim the victory until she'd crossed the porch, navigated the dark interior and managed to safely fall into bed versus falling flat on her face between here and her goal. She wanted to sleep until she felt rested. It would probably be days. Unfortunately, that option was off the table. She'd get her gear together and hit the road tomorrow as soon as she'd had enough sleep so she could be sure she was safe to drive. When she got to her mom's house, she'd hibernate. Or hide. They sounded oddly similar.

There was just enough light in the little house that she could make her way to the bedroom with nothing more than a stubbed toe. But standing there in front of the fluffy bed with its practical yet pretty bedding, she couldn't force herself to crawl in. She was caked in dirt and sweat and saddle oil and horse hair.

And him.

Riding home together, she'd been pressed to Quinn's chest. If she moved just right, she could smell him. Faint, but there.

Shower it was.

Every move she made was one of muscle memory—bathing, shampooing, conditioning, rinsing. The routine was comfortable, but that created its own problem. Because she didn't have to think about what she was doing, it left her mind to wander, and she couldn't keep her mind from going places she longed to explore yet feared to tread.

But I remembered.

She'd only retrieved a short snapshot of that day—hard fast images and sharp sounds—but it had been more than she'd possessed before. Somehow, it had been—was—too much and not nearly enough.

What she'd said to Quinn in the little demi-cave had been absolutely true. She wanted to remember in order to honor the men who had died. Just as much, she needed to know that she'd done right by them that day, that she hadn't made a bad call. It wouldn't have been the first time. Not that she was some rebellious risk taker, especially when it came to the lives of her crew. But there had been a few times when she and her crew had straddled the go/no-go line, that point where she made the call to push on or turn back.

Taylor wasn't one to give up, get beat down or quit. And turning back from a rescue call, something she saw as the result of a direct challenge from Mother Nature, sometimes tasted too much like just that. Quitting.

Her men had followed her as a result of the way she pushed, her drive, her teasing phrase that had become their motto: "If Mother Nature thinks she's going to own me today, that bitch better bring more money to the table." While there had been some calls they got a little beat *up* on, they were never beat*en*. Big difference. Huge.

If she'd made the call to go that day, the call that sent them to their deaths, they would have followed her. Period.

Taylor shut the shower off, stepped out and made brisk work of drying off. She should have taken the time to review her new bruise collection, but that would require some twisting and turning and checking herself out in the mirror. No, thanks. She'd taught herself to avoid looking in the mirror when she didn't have to and to focus on narrow points when she had no other options—makeup, firsthand first aid, etc. Bruises weren't sufficient reason to break her truce with herself. Looking at what remained of her body…hurt. More than she'd ever thought it would. She wasn't vain or arrogant. Truly. But she didn't recognize or, worse, empathize, with the woman who stared back at her.

Total. Stranger.

The Taylor Williams she knew would never have let her friends die.

Lethargy stole over her and left her limbs impossibly heavy and her heart even more so. Running a brush through her hair was the best she could do. Drying that mop wasn't happening. She was tapped out. Tomorrow was a travel day anyway, so she'd shove the mass up under her hat before she left.

Shutting the light off in the bathroom, she gave her eyes a moment to adjust before she blindly felt her way into the bedroom. She folded the covers back and, still wrapped in her towel, crawled into bed. It was too much effort to pull the covers up, so she lay on her side and curled an arm under her head for support. She'd put her pajamas on in a minute.

Honest.

Right now, all she wanted to do was stare out the picture window at the radiant stars that peppered the blue-black of the night sky. Her grandpa had once told her the stars were wishes people had made, wishes that were waiting for the right time to come true.

A brilliant flash streaked across the darkness.

A falling star.

A *dying* star.

"That one belonged to me, Gramps," she whispered. So many things she had wished for over the years were still waiting to happen. But some wishes never came true, like wishing for a do-over the day of the accident. Or wishing she could make a different first impression with Quinn. Wishing they could have met under different circumstances when they were both different people. The people they'd been before tragedy stole those who were irreplaceable from each of them. Things might have been different. A hot tear traced over cool skin and disappeared into the hair at her temple.

Sleep's persistent pull encouraged her to close her eyes, and she did.

As beautiful as that endless night sky was, she just couldn't bear to watch any more wishes fall to their deaths tonight.

QUINN HADN'T ARGUED with Taylor ditching him before they hit the barn. His need to sort his head out trumped his desire for her. At least, it *had*. But the longer she was gone, the longer he was stuck with only himself and the animals for company, the worse things got. He wanted to turn horses and donkey out to pasture and follow the woman who had left him astride his horse as if she slipped away into the proverbial sunset every chance she had.

"Not this time, sunshine." He was vigorous in his brushing of coats and cleaning of feet.

Cob nudged him and huffed a breath that followed the hollow of Quinn's spine right down the back of his jeans and cooled the sweat that slicked his body, head to toe.

Shooing the annoying jack away, Quinn finished with Jigsaw, stabled him for the night and then turned his attention to Amante. The animal had thrown a shoe sometime during the adventure and was favoring that front foot. The hoof looked okay, but he figured he might as well call Doc Tolbert. The last thing the ranch needed was a huge vet bill. At the same time, though, the ranch couldn't afford to have one of their best working horses come up lame right before they held their cattle branding.

He put the horses up for the night and saw them fed and watered. Then, with his mind preoccupied managing rapid-fire worries—the cost of the potential vet bill, anticipated yearling prices in the sale ring, what he figured they'd make versus what it would take to settle the bank note that was fast coming due—he dialed the doctor. And didn't pay much attention as the phone rang. And rang. And rang. Impatience crept up on him, turning his attention to the screen at the same time the vet answered.

"It's after dinner, after dark and you're interrupting my date. If no one's dying, I'm going to ask if this can wait until morning."

Quinn glanced at the phone a second time. Yep. He'd called the right number. "Doc?"

"You're the one dialed my number. Don't sound so surprised I'm the one that answered."

"I've got a small problem out here at the Rocking-B."

"Quinn?" The vet he'd known all his life suddenly sounded rattled. "You okay? What's wrong? You're not hurt are you?"

"It's Quinn? What's wrong?" a female voice demanded. The rustle of covers and what sounded like bare feet hitting the floor closed in on the phone. "Let me talk to him, Sam. Quinn? It's Mom. What's wrong?"

Shock flat laid him out, stealing his voice in the process. And it was a good thing, too. Had he let loose with the tirade, shouts, denials and accusations that erupted in rapid-fire succession in his head and were now running amok, he had no doubt his mother would have come home and washed his mouth out with soap. The odds of him ever being "too grown" for that were hella-slim to flat-out *none*, and she'd never made any bones about it. He wheezed, the sound not unlike an old engine trying to get enough air to get going.

"Why are you calling Sam so late? Tell me what happened," his mother demanded, the sharp snap of her directive zinging through him and making him instinctively stand up straight. "You answer me right now, son. Do I need to come home? Taylor—she's okay?"

"No! Yes." He didn't have the wherewithal to face his mother right now. Especially not after this little revelation. "You don't need to come home. Taylor is…she's probably enjoying a hot shower if she hasn't gone to bed already." *Truth.*

Betrayal ached at the heart of everything he was, and part of him knew he wasn't being fair. The other part?

Yeah. He needed time to level out so he didn't say something that would hurt his mom. Nothing, *nothing*, would be worse than that.

He couldn't make sense of the level of his rage. For the last year and a half, he'd been the one to pick up the pieces for his mom, try to hold the ranch together and keep food on the table and in the troughs. He'd worked his ass off to keep the wolves at bay, and it hadn't been enough.

If Quinn wasn't strong enough to keep the ranch together and afford his mom the security of home and hearth, how the hell was he *ever* going to offer that, and more, to Taylor?

Gripping the phone like it was Sam Tolbert's neck, Quinn paced and worked to measure the pitch and volume of every word. "Well, this is awkward, *Mom*."

"This isn't the way I wanted this topic to come up, but what's done is done. I'm going to say this one time, Quinn. Tread lightly here. Snap judgments are far more likely to bite you in the ass than they are to win you any wars. I'll take a lot from the boy I know is hurting, but I won't take a single ugly word off the man who was raised better than to cast stones." Her words were even, measured and cool.

Throat tight, he managed a small sound he hoped fell under "humor" but more likely landed square in the middle of he-who-lacks-common-courtesy. He cleared his throat and tried again. "I believe it would be best if I talk to Sam."

"You and I will sort this out tomorrow."

Something primal rose up in Quinn, something that demanded he protect and cherish and nurture and defend all at the same time. "You do what you need to do, and I'll do the same. Put Sam on the phone, Mom. Please."

She huffed and handed over the phone, an unintelligible exchange occurring between the two before Sam's voice came on. "This isn't how I wanted to go about this with you either, Quinn."

He blew out a sharp breath. "I'm going to assume it would be better for us to deal with this when we've all had some time to decide how we're going to handle it. I, for one, need a chance to cool off so I don't say something that would hurt my mother. That means that until, you know, the year 2073, I'm going to pretend I called and told you that my gelding, Amante, had thrown a shoe and was limping. You responded with…"

"Questions. Any visible swelling in the pastern, fetlock, cannon or knee? Any heat in the joints?" The man's voice was professional, kind and compassionate. Familiar. And Quinn resented Sam for that as much as anything, that it was this other man's voice on the end of the line and not his dad's. It was this impossible-to-define reminder that, short of a couple of voicemails he'd inadvertently saved and a few home movies, Quinn would never hear his dad's voice again.

That wouldn't be true with Sam. The veterinarian was right there, taking up the place his dad should never have vacated. The place his dad *would* have been in, if Quinn had been even half as loyal as his old man. But he hadn't. He'd been selfish, seizing the opportunity his dad had presented him with all those years ago, the chance to get out of Crooked Water and do more, *be* more, than a rancher's son. In the end, his selfishness had cost his dad his life.

"Quinn?" Sam prompted.

"No swelling, no heat," he replied woodenly.

Sam made a positive noise, sort of an "mm-hmm-good-mm-hmm" that ran together. The sound was likely meant to be encouraging and probably would have been—to a client who wasn't so enraged that he could boil an egg by spitting on its shell.

"How long has the horse been shod, and are the shoes new or old?"

"Shoes are about three weeks old. I've kept all the horses shod and done the farrier work myself," Quinn said with deceptive casualness. "You know, just like Dad taught me to do as a kid, long before he died."

"No need to remind me, Quinn. Anyone and everyone who knew your dad mourned his passing. That includes me."

As far as cool management of his backhanded and intentionally unkind comment went, Quinn had to give the guy props.

Point to the vet.

Sam continued in the same calm, professional voice, though it was a little less friendly. "Chances are good that, after the animal threw the shoe, he crossed rough ground. He probably stepped on all kinds of crap that would have pressed against the parts of the hoof, sole and frog that the shoe had protected. I'd be willing to bet he's just tender footed and will be fine in a day or two. If not, I'll take a look."

"So, is that the equivalent of 'have him take two Tylenol and call me in the morning'?" Quinn asked through clenched teeth.

"Pretty much." Gone was any attempt at putting up an easygoing front. Sam knew Quinn well enough to be wary.

Smart man.

"Excellent. I'll do just that." He knew he should leave it alone. Knew he had no business intervening in his mother's life any more than he did Taylor's, but both women were essentially in his keeping at the moment, and if his dad had taught him anything, it was that you do whatever you have to do to take care of your own.

Quinn's psyche had armored up throughout the shallow exchange and was fully prepared for war. He could almost see it hop off its steady steed, Common Sense, and, with a stone-cold countenance, charge into the fray wielding his multitalented weapon of choice, known to his enemies as Can o' Whoopass. "Thanks for the advice. I'd appreciate it if you'd make sure the bill comes to my attention.

"As a courtesy, I'm going to give you a little advice of my own. You touch my mother in any way she doesn't explicitly ask for—and I blame you for the nightmares I'm going to have over just that—and I will come for you, Sam. I don't give a ripe rat's ass that you're my elder or were one of Dad's closest friends. Or you were supposed to be, anyway."

"Just a minute—" Sam fired back with what Quinn thought was probably justifiable outrage.

Justified or not, it didn't give Quinn even a moment's pause and he carried on like Sam hadn't spoken. "No, Sam. *You* hold on. That woman, the one who's either in your bed or the one you're working to get there? Sure, she's a grown woman, but she's all I've got. You'd better believe I'd move heaven and earth to see her safe. I would face down hell's own army if it meant sparing that amazing lady a single ounce of additional hurt in her lifetime. That makes you—a country vet with a damn good education, a nicer work truck than we can afford and a waistline sporting more than five decades of home-cooked meals—about as insignificant as a horsefly on a sow's back as far as I'm concerned."

Quinn disconnected the call, shoved his phone in his pocket and turned three tight circles before he hauled back and punched the tack-room door as hard as he could. Two more strikes and his knuckles were split and dripping blood like a garden hose under high pressure.

It didn't happen very often that he botched up everything he laid hands on in a day. So, while today might be the exception, it still sucked.

He started across the field toward home, mind on a hundred thousand things, trying to go a million different ways. A coyote howled, the sound clear and bright, and he looked up to see if he could catch a glimpse of the animal. They shouldn't be this close to the house. He'd have to make sure he had his rifle with him and talk to Taylor about safety precautions if she went out at night. Of course, with her experience at Rainier, she'd know how to…

He stopped and looked over at the dark cottage. Not even a single light burned. It made sense she would have gone to bed early, seeing as her intent was to pack up and bug out.

He imagined her in the cottage, doing what she'd said she was going to do—shower and sleep. Rather, his *intention* had been to consider her advertised actions. He didn't make it past her getting into the shower. Ghostlike images of her rose from his memory, eyes bright, hair wild, skin flushed with passion. He'd roused that in her and hadn't needed a mirror to know she'd done the same to him. The interruption caused by the revival of her past and the appearance of his prejudice had really messed up what might have been a very good thing.

He took one step, then another and suddenly he was walking toward the cottage.

She lied to me.

He stopped.

Not exactly true. She put down all of her information as it was correct in that moment, even the Virginia address. So where's the lie? If I didn't realize she was the captain from the Rainier wreck, that's on me. It's not fair to hold her responsible for ensuring I made the connection between her infamy and her address.

He took a hesitant step toward the cabin, and then stopped. Again.

She wasn't forthcoming about her panic attacks. I'm not a doctor, so I'm not sure what they mean as far as her stability. And she did include medical clearance that said she was physically fit to make the climb. That paperwork fulfilled the requirements I have on my site. Every one of them. And she didn't hesitate to provide them.

He began walking toward the cabin again, steps slower, more thoughtful.

The woman has been stared at and whispered about and her judgment made the topic of open conjecture. She's handled it with grace and quiet strength. If I question that, am I being as judgmental as the rest of the climbing world?

He sped up.

If I knock on her door, and if she opens it, we'll both know why I'm there.

He was jogging now.

I have felt more alive in her company, more present in any given moment, than I've felt since my phone rang the night Dad died. And when she kissed me?

He wasn't sprinting. Not by definition. But that was only because no one was there to argue semantics with him.

A tiny flare above the cabin caught his attention and shifted his focus off the front door.

Shooting star.

Its tail burned bright against the inky night sky, that light a silent demand someone recognize it before it was lost.

Seized by spontaneity, Quinn did something he hadn't done in too many years to count.

He made a wish.

Complex in many ways and fundamentally simple in many others, every component of the wish shared a single foundation.

Hope.

12

TAYLOR'S FIRST SCREAM was tearing up the airwaves before
consciousness registered and she realized she'd made any
sound at all. The crash of the door being kicked in happened as she drew in a breath and let her second scream
loose, this one not a result of a nightmare but rather the
man rushing into her room. The pitch and volume was
equivalent to a tornado siren. Quinn ran into the room
and moved stealthily along the walls as he sought out the
threat. Both hands were up and at the ready like a prize
fighter. Then? The look on his face said it was *on*.

Her scream faded to a whimper and was gone, the remaining silence heavy.

He circled back around to her and stopped dead in his
tracks. The night was bright and cast enough light on his
face that she could see the changes in him, going from
attack-maul-maim-murder to something that might have
been more dangerous to her in particular, something that
purred want-pleasure-hunger-possess…repeat. Her legs
went weak at the promise of the last. It was all she could
do to keep from breaking out in a sweat from the heated
impact of his gaze on her bare skin.

Bare…skin…

The small *eep* that escaped her couldn't be taken back any more than she could cover her entire body, head to toe, to change the way he continued to drink her in. Those big, greedy gulps left far more than just her limbs exposed. The way he looked at her was like he saw through her and into the very heart of who she was. And if the bulging length behind the zipper of his jeans was anything to go by, he wasn't exactly disappointed with the skin show.

Skin.

If anything was going to get her moving, the idea that she was nearly naked in front of him would be at the top of that list.

"Quinn," she said on a shallow breath, going to her knees and reaching for his shirt. Gripping it in handfuls. Pulling him to her. Looking up into his shadowed face. Pleading without shame. Without any intent to regret. Rising up, laying her lips to the corner of his mouth. "I need… Please. Help me chase away the darkness."

He turned a fraction and his lips closed over hers in a tender but possessive couldn't-be-denied crush, drawing in her breath and the small noises of pleading she made, noises she wasn't sure were in protest of the kiss or protesting that he might consider stopping. He swallowed every one of them until it felt like she'd been consumed by his heat, claimed in some primal way and branded in a very contemporary fashion. None of it bothered her in the least.

She realized then that she'd snaked her arms up his chest. One hand had wadded his T-shirt up and she clung to the fabric like it was her life vest in this emotional storm. She wound her other arm around his neck and tunneled her fingers through his hair. It was the perfect combination of pressure and friction, as crazed and delicious as it was forbidden and necessary. Pressure between their torsos was all that kept the towel from puddling at their feet. Panicked, she shifted and the towel started to slip. She twisted and tried to break away, curling in on herself.

He wasn't having it, though. Quinn turned and, keeping a firm grip on her, gently shoved her down on the bed. He followed, pinning her beneath him when he draped one leg over her upper thighs. Reclaiming her hand, he gripped her wrist and, peeling her hand open, laid it over his jackhammering heart. A tender kiss, words whispered against her lips, words that meant more by tone than by definition.

Pushing up on one elbow, he hovered over her, his smile composed of a thousand things she wanted to hear him say, his lips tempting in their own right. A swift kiss and then his gaze settled on the towel, his finger teasing the edge. "Drop that towel, brave woman." Another kiss. "For me." A kiss lower. "Please." A kiss at the hollow of her neck. "I want to finish what we started this afternoon, Taylor. I want all of you. Every inch. The scars? They're ribbons, the hard-earned marks of a survivor who fought her way back from the abyss. Don't hide them. Not from me."

Taylor couldn't think. She swam through the thick emotions clogging her mind, half of which made her feel quietly shy and the other half sexually primed. "I don't share the scars, Quinn. I never have. Not unless the request comes from a doctor or therapist."

"Or me." Tracing her lower lip with his thumb, he went quiet.

She got more nervous, running her fingers up and down the edge of the towel. Fine sweat dotted her upper lip and spots swam across her vision. *Can I do this?* Where faith and fear collided, a kernel of new hope was born, anchored in the small divide separating them—a divide that grew smaller with every little kindness, every tender word and every gesture of goodwill.

With hands that shook like fall leaves in a stiff wind, Taylor pulled the towel free.

Silence ruled every bit of space between them until that chasm started to grow and the comfort diminished, and Taylor wondered what in the world she'd been thinking to let him this close to her, to let him see her exposed in a way that would be irrecoverable. After all, a person couldn't unsee what the mind saw and understood.

She was preparing to launch herself out of his reach when Quinn laid his whole hand over her abdomen and said in an awed voice, "You are fierce, Taylor Williams."

Darkness clouded the edges of her vision. "Make me forget what it is to feel too much."

The strangest look passed over the cowboy's face. "I can do that."

"What can I do for you?"

"Just keep being you."

QUINN TRIED NOT to stare at the crisscross patterns over Taylor's flat stomach. One of the hard lines cut right through her belly button. For some reason, that scar, and not the one that was as thick as his little finger, was the one that bothered him the most. He followed it down to the edge of the towel that lay at her side. The ribbon of scar disappeared.

She worried her lower lip. "Do they bother you?"

He took her face in his hands and reignited the kiss between them, the energy as rich and powerful as it had been the first time he'd put his mouth to hers and every bit as intoxicating as the last. She tasted the same as she had before, of sunshine and evergreen, and she made him want to fall into her and stay there.

Fall into her...

While the sentiment had been sincere, carnal images overloaded his circuitry.

Going to his knees, he ripped his shirt over his head and rested his hand on the button at his waist. "This call has to be yours, Taylor. It probably seems simple, and I guess in a lot of ways it is. But we're talking about more than a night. At least, for me." He kept his voice calm, his tone straightforward. "I want to see what this thing is."

"This call? I don't know. Quinn, I don't know." Her hands moved absently to shield her bare breasts and then went back to cover her belly. Chances were good she didn't even know she did it. Then she curled away just enough to shield herself. "What thing?" she finally asked, not meeting his eyes when she reached for the very edge of the towel in a rudimentary attempt to cover up. He intercepted her effort and she sighed, wrapping her arms around her middle.

"Stay for your climb. You need the recertification and I need…" He hesitated. The honest answer was twofold: the climb fee and her. He needed both. Weighing the consequences, he gave her part of the answer, just as she'd given him. "I need you to give this thing between us a shot while you're here. Let's see what it really is." Reaching out, he stroked her wild-woman curls from her face. "A week, Taylor. Give me a week."

She slid a glance at him. "And then what? Either way, then what?"

"We either part as friends or we find a way to remain lovers." He popped the button on his jeans, his erection throbbing with this elemental need he had for her. The heat in her eyes gave him hope.

Taylor's attention became hyperfocused on his jeans. She licked her lips and blinked up at him. "You promise to be as hard on me in the re-cert as you have a reputation for being. No cutting me any slack just because you're—" she trailed a finger down the valley between his abs "—*in* my slacks."

Quinn laughed right up to the point she curled her fingers over the top of the ridge of his jeans. Short, blunt nails tenderly raked across the swollen head of his cock, tracing through the moisture that gathered there and spreading it around. His hips bucked, every bit of him anxious for more of her touch. Yanking down the zipper on his Wranglers, he shoved the denim to his hips.

His erection sprang from a midnight thatch at the hilt. He widened his stance as much as he could, given the half-on, half-off jeans.

He shouted something unintelligible when she dragged the flat of her tongue over the broad head of his erection and traced the tip as she went. *Definitely* taste him. That was *so* on the two-for-twenty breakfast, lunch and dinner menus they'd be sharing.

She rolled away with controlled care until she finally lay on her back, casually tossing one arm above her head while she stroked him from root to tip with her free hand. Those magic fingers stilled and she looked up at him. "I haven't said yes."

Lacing his hands behind his neck, he pulled tight, locking them together. "If this is your version of no, I'm going to give you reason to say it as often as possible."

"Don't hurt me, Quinn." The words seemed to escape her in an embarrassing rush. "I just..." She waved him off, rolled her head to the side and stared out the window again.

"Honesty, Taylor. Now and always." Toeing off first his boots and then his jeans, he crawled in naked beside her. "I am going into this with eyes wide open and absolutely no intent to cause you any harm. This is my visual of going all in. You?"

She looked at him, steady and considering. A slow smile spread over her face.

Bumblebees bounced around inside his belly, alternately tickling his insides before stinging the crap out of him. "Taylor?"

"I'm willing to give it a shot. But Quinn? If I'm the one 'going in' in this rodeo, sex is going to be awkward. You're totally built to be in." She looked up at him and her smile widened. "I'm more your wide receiver."

"Yeah?" He knelt in the cradle of her legs. "You're part of every play. Incoming."

Retrieving a condom from his wallet, he slid it down his length.

Taylor made a small, needful sound that reeled Quinn in more efficiently than a deep-sea fisherman pulling in a prize catch.

Falling forward onto one hand, he used his free hand to trace the outer swell of her closest breast, reveling in the pearling nipple and sounds of hunger that followed.

Shifting as he lowered his hips, he placed the swollen head of his arousal against her slickened sex. Heartbeat after heartbeat made his cock rise and fall, teasing her clitoris with light strokes that had her whimpering. Those sounds unraveled Quinn, threatening to undo him where he lay.

"Not happening," he whispered.

Reaching between their bodies, he pulled back and pinched the base of his shaft. He wouldn't lose it and embarrass himself. Not this first time. He was too desperate to feel her, to experience the pressure of her walls gripping him as he inched his way into the very heart of her, the source of her heat. Her center.

Seeming to realize he was trying to regain control, the little vixen gripped his shaft and gave a slow, sensuous pull.

He was a slave to her desire and his, unable and unwilling to deny either of them the culmination of their attraction. Moreover, he couldn't turn away from this unyielding, ever-present hunger he had for this woman, a hunger that was as emotional as it was physical. It had been present when they met, growing like a wild, living thing.

"Quinn." His name was on her breath again, this time infused with a whole new level of desire.

He knew he'd be humbled later when he replayed their physical joining, but right now? All he could do was follow her direction and give her what she wanted.

Wrapping his hand around hers, they worked together to guide his length and girth to her opening. The fit was tight, almost impossibly so, and he paused when she arched her back and gasped.

He stilled. "Talk to me, Taylor. Tell me what you need."

"Don't you dare quit, Quinn." She curled her hips toward him, the movement sharp and fast, taking him in another two inches all at once. Her inner walls squeezed once, hard, then seemed to welcome him as they stretched to accommodate the invasion and draw him in.

He slid the last three inches with a shout, seating himself to the root.

Instinct refused to let him pair mind and body, demanding he withdraw and then drive home, the action a repetitive primal need. Truly, he tried for control, but nothing had ever felt so good—until she found the rhythm of their bodies and began to thrust her hips up to meet his descent.

Skin slapped against sweat-slicked skin, the noise an erotic background that accompanied his nonsensical words of praise and her small mewls of pleasure and pleas of, "More!" and "Harder!" and "There! Sweet heaven, *right there*!"

Reaching between them once more, he found her swollen clit and, with his thumb, finessed the little knot as he leaned in, hips still pumping, and said, "Come for me, Taylor. Come for me *now*."

Lifting himself up on his other arm, he watched her face, eyes wide, as he pinched and pulled the very source guaranteed to bring her over.

She clawed at the sheets. Her legs wound around him. Then her mouth formed a small O a split second before she arched her back and shouted his name.

Quinn's own release roared toward him, racing up his spine and down, drawing his sac up tight. But that wasn't what made him utter her name with sheer reverence. Her name on his lips came from a deeper place, somewhere no lover had ever trod. As her walls squeezed and stroked him, and his orgasm closed in, what took him over was the realization that this was the first time he'd ever experienced an emotional connection of this magnitude. His heart was laid bare before her in abject supplication, an offering if she would have it. And he hoped to God she would.

Words left him entirely as his orgasm seized him then, dragging him into the abyss into which she'd already fallen.

He'd never been so grateful to fall, and in more ways than one.

13

TAYLOR CRAWLED OUT of bed while the sky was still pink with dawn. Quinn had kissed her goodbye about thirty minutes ago, saying something about chores and reminding her to make it to breakfast today. She'd nodded and pointed him to a door. Turned out it had been the closet door, but hey, when a woman was this sexually blissed out? He was lucky she'd managed to find a door at all.

It took her about twenty minutes to pull herself together. More than once she grinned, amused at all the sore spots because, truthfully, from jaw to toes, every muscle ached. Managing the steps made her groan and laugh at the same time. What she'd shared with Quinn last night had changed everything for her. She could only hope he'd experienced something similar.

Emotions had aligned in a way that helped her find her true center, a place that had been a foreign emotional landscape to her since the accident.

And, in the very heart of her self, she knew last night hadn't left her the only one affected. More than once she'd caught Quinn watching her with an undisguised passion that ran deeper than the simple joining of two bodies. What they'd shared amounted to far more than sex. But she still needed to hear him offer her the affirmation she craved, to give her a place to belong again, and she wanted, *needed*, that place to be at his side.

Taylor couldn't survive another heartbreak that reduced her to a party of one. So she would tread carefully but without giving in to the mind-numbing fear that had weighed her down for so long. She would give Quinn time to navigate the maze of emotions and give voice to what had been born between them.

Lifting her face to the morning sun, she took a deep breath that finally satisfied. Then she headed toward the main house, her step lighter, her heart harboring a terrifying but buoyant kernel of that elusive thing called hope.

Smoke drifted in lazy spires from the old stone chimney, the occasional belch of sparks flashing bright before burning away. The smell of frying bacon hit her when her boot-clad foot settled on the first stair tread, the aroma like an elixir that summoned her forward more effectively than a preacher calling his congregation forward at the end of a Sunday sermon. She made it halfway across the deep front porch before she realized there was a dog—a *big* dog—lying on the porch mat.

The animal bared its teeth and stopped Taylor in her tracks. Then the thing thumped its tail in a motorboat manner created by wagging its tail in a rapid circular motion and pairing the movement with a rumbly growl.

She didn't know what to do, and options were slim. If she stood there trying not to get mauled before her first cup of coffee, she'd miss breakfast altogether. If she moved forward, she'd have to put herself in proximity to those teeth in order to knock on the door and, consequently, get her caffeine fix. And bacon. After experiencing Quinn last night, she *needed* bacon. No, she had *earned* her bacon.

Apparently she'd stood there long enough that the dog

felt compelled to act. The animal rose and shuffled toward her, head low and teeth bared even as its tail did its impression of a motorboat. Ironically, the closer it got to her, the faster its tail went and the more enamel it exposed with its growl.

Taylor slowly moved back toward the steps.

Elaine passed in front of a large window and must have caught Taylor's movement. The other woman took in the scene at hand and rushed for the front door, yanking it open.

"Gravy!" she snapped.

The dog whipped around, its tail now a blur of happy motion.

"Stop screwing around," Elaine admonished. "You'll scare someone to death if you keep on with that toothy grin."

"That *grin*?" Taylor wheezed.

"He's four and probably the only black Labrador *retriever* that thinks he's supposed to retrieve cattle, not fowl." She shook her head, her long hair loose around her shoulders. "He's also criminally social. I imagine he'd welcome a stranger into the house if we weren't here. And if a c-o-o-k-i-e was involved, he'd show the thief where the money and guns are kept." Gravy's ears perked, his bright eyes locked on Elaine. "And, yes, I have to spell around my dog, though he's catching on to that, too. Hold on." Disappearing for a second, she popped back onto the porch with a thick-cut slice of bacon. "Sit."

"Me or Gravy?" Taylor asked. "Because for bacon? I'll sit, roll over or play dead. Your call." Elaine's subsequent laughter was a spiritual buoy, a place in which Taylor found a surprising sense of safety and security. Comfort, even. "How do you do that?" she asked with unabashed curiosity.

"Do what?"

Taylor snapped out of her little reverie and shook her head. "Nothing. Forget it. May I help with breakfast?"

"All I have left is sweet milk gravy and that all but makes itself." Elaine openly considered Taylor. "What were you referring to when you asked how I 'do that'? Do what, exactly?"

Taylor stared at the ground, toying with the bottom button of her sleeveless denim shirt. *How to answer?* There were an infinite number of ways she could've worded her response, but the simple truth was always her first choice. Drawing a deep breath, she looked up and met Elaine's gaze. "How do you make an uncomfortable situation feel, well, basically comfortable?"

Elaine's face softened. "I'm a mom, honey. It's part of the job description."

Taylor didn't bother disguising her amusement. "My mom has a different job and, consequently, a different job description."

Holding the door wide, Elaine waited for Taylor to enter before responding. "I suppose each woman approaches parenting differently." She pulled a large jar of flour from a cabinet and set about making gravy. "What does your mom do?"

"She's a drug lord during the day and serves several weekends and two main events a year as the grand poobah to the board of directors for a children's charity." At Elaine's confused look, Taylor sank into a chair at the counter and propped her chin on her hand. "Chief executive officer for a pharmaceutical company and the chairperson of the board of directors for a national children's charity. She works a lot."

"What about your dad?"

"He used to run an East Coast investment group. He's

since retired so he could find himself. Who knew his spirit was trapped in his golf bag?" She smiled.

Working a few tablespoons of flour into her cast iron skillet, Elaine didn't turn around when she asked, "Are you close to your family?"

The question didn't require thought. "Not by any stretch of the imagination. My brother is their perfect trust-fund-baby-who-has-it-all-together-and-got-it-all-right golden-child. I'm…" She laughed, the sound bitter even to her. "Let's just leave it at no, we're not close."

She sat up straight and rested her forearms on the butcher-block counter. "What about you? Do you have a great relationship with each of your children?"

Elaine glanced back and offered a quick smile. "Quinn's an only child. Complications with his pregnancy meant I couldn't have more after him."

"I'm sorry."

"Don't be. I'm thrilled I have him." She paused, strain showing at the corners of her eyes. For a second Taylor thought she was going to add something else about Quinn, but she shook her head and went back to cooking. "He's always been an amazing kid."

"Of course I have," said the man under discussion.

Quinn padded into the kitchen in jeans, a long-sleeved shirt and sock feet. Dark hair still damp from the shower curled around his nape. The scent of his soap, rich and clean, wasn't strong enough to override that of the bacon, but it still skated across the air and teased Taylor's nose. He glanced at her then, his eyes hooded, heavy, satiated. With a wink, he reached around his mom's arm and snagged a piece of bacon. "I got most of the chores done but still need to get the horses out of the barn. Is there time before we eat or should I wait?"

"It won't hurt them to wait." The woman neither paused

nor looked up from the task at hand but still managed to rap his knuckles with her spoon. "And you know better than that, young man. Ladies first. To think I was just bragging on you."

"Hey, now. I'm a good kid." His protest opened the door to a bantering exchange.

Taylor only half listened. She couldn't fathom having a relationship like that with her parents. First, her mother *didn't* cook. She *had* a cook. The idea of Madison Williams standing over a hot stove and dealing with bacon grease in her Chanel boggled Taylor's mind.

Second, her dad getting up in time for breakfast hadn't happened in too long to remember. Lunch? Sure. But breakfast hours didn't fit with his personal habits, in particular his penchant for late nights, bottomless bar tabs and repetitive hangovers. He'd evolved literally overnight, going from the rigid-yet-absent tyrant of her childhood to an equally uninvolved, intentionally absent retiree. His solution to everything was to throw money at it, and she was an "it" in his book. He'd ensured her bank account was sufficiently funded yet he'd never once made a deposit in her emotional portfolio.

Quinn had, though.

A slight chill skipped down her spine at the realization that, once again, she was waiting for that deposit slip—the words that had always been denied her.

And, right then, she hated her father for the person he'd trained her to be, a person who wanted more than anything the one thing money couldn't buy.

Love.

THE SECOND QUINN had stepped out of the little cottage, he'd begun looking forward to seeing Taylor again. He'd rushed through chores in the hope he could get in a shower before she showed up. Mission accomplished. What he *hadn't* counted on was that his mom would come back so early following *her* little slumber party. They were dancing around each other now, trying to figure out how they should behave with each other. And, honestly? Seeing her had fanned his anger. It wasn't that he didn't want his mom to be happy. It just seemed like there should be some kind of fixed time limit that had to be spent grieving before she was out...*dating*. She was dating, not having...

"If you're going to stand there flirting like a seventeen-year-old debate team captain with a Clearasil habit, step out of the traffic flow, Quinn." His mom winked at him. "Otherwise, grab the stuff to set the table. We're almost ready to eat."

He shook his head and found he'd indeed been standing there, slack-jawed, as he stared at Taylor again.

He. Was. Awesome.

Then she gave him a little finger wave behind his mom's back and he bought into his own hype.

Watching Taylor's face go twelve graduated shades of red made it worth it, but it was very hard not to snark back at his mom.

"You want coffee, orange juice, milk or a combination?" His question was met with silence. Glancing over his shoulder, he found her watching his mom make gravy. "Taylor?"

She jerked around, blinked rapidly. "Sorry. What?"

Elaine smiled in her direction. "What do you want to drink, honey?"

"Milk." The answer sounded surprisingly small.

Quinn grabbed the gallon and the juice pitcher, set them on the table and then poured everyone coffee. "How do you take yours, Taylor?"

This time she did look at him. "I don't drink coffee."

He stilled. "Excuse me?"

"I don't—"

"He heard you. Coffee's nearly a religion out here. He got that from his dad." An odd look passed over his mom's face, her mind obviously elsewhere when she absently gestured toward the table. "Have a seat, Taylor. I'm sure that, if you give him a minute to adjust his world view, he'll stop standing there like a simpleton. Quinn, man the gravy. I'll be back in a few minutes and we'll eat."

He picked up the whisk and shot his mom a sharp look, but she only shook her head and walked out the back door. She did this on occasion, fleeing the house when some uninvited memory shook her. If he followed her, she'd get irritated at having her grief witnessed. His mom was a strong woman, but a broken heart was a broken heart.

"Everything okay?"

Taylor's question pulled him into the moment. "It'll be fine." He stirred the gravy, added a little milk and stirred some more. The silence between them grew heavy before settling between his shoulders and making his skin twitch like that of a nervous horse. God help him if bolting didn't sound fine right about then. There had to be something safe to talk about.

"I'm impressed you can cook."

Her voice came from immediately behind him. Startled, he splashed a glob of gravy on the burner. Fingers of smoke curled up from the hot eye seconds before the pungent smell of burning grease and flour struck him. Waving at the smoke, he turned up the oven exhaust and then cringed at the smoke alarm's screech. Something crashed behind him. He spun and found Taylor, eyes the size of saucers and skin the color of cream, dragging the stool toward the zealous alarm.

She parked the stool directly below and scrambled up,

stretching as far as she could to pull the battery. Her reach was about six inches short. That's when she began to shake. Violently.

"Taylor?" He pushed the pan to a cool burner before crossing the room in several long strides. "Baby, what's wrong?" He reached for her.

She flinched, her gaze darting around before coming to rest on his. Terror glazed her eyes and confirmed that, while she might be looking at him, it wasn't him she saw. Just like yesterday, the trauma of the accident and the subsequent loss had hit her hard.

A fat tear slipped down her cheek and she shuddered.

"I'm going to get you down, okay?" No response. He reached for her again, ignoring her flinch as he settled his hands firmly at her waist. She was tall but lean, so lifting her off the stool was easy. Managing her weight when she consequently flung herself at him and clung like premium shrink-wrap? Not so much.

His arms instinctively went around her, one under her butt for support and the other slipping up her back to cradle her head, encouraging her cheek to his shoulder. They crashed to the floor in a tangle of limbs, Quinn twisting at the last minute to spare her the impact.

The alarm blared on.

"I'm going to feel that one tomorrow."

The backdoor crashed against the mudroom wall, and then his mother was there. Gravy was at her side, the hair down his back bristling as he sought out the threat. Seeing Quinn and Taylor on the floor, the dog did his creepy grin thing, then bounded over and immediately set to licking their faces with joyful abandon.

Quinn protested with sharp, loud language.

Taylor didn't object. At all.

Please don't let her have hit her head.

Images of all the things that could have gone wrong began to race through his head, and fear began to color everything he saw, everything he thought, everything he felt.

"A little help here?" he shouted, twisting left and right, tucking his chin as he tried to keep the dog's tongue out of his mouth. "Back off, Gravy! I can only say no so many times before I have to take your harassment to management. Have a little pride, man."

His mom paused for a split second and seemed to take everything in—two adults wrapped around each other on the floor, the screeching alarm, Taylor's full-body trembles, the French-kissing canine, the smell of something burning. Then she erupted into a whirlwind of activity. Grabbing the broom, she climbed onto the stool Taylor had parked beneath the alarm and beat the offending appliance like it was a piñata filled with gold bullion. Plastic shattered, the alarm's casing spattering across the ground in jagged pieces, but the sound didn't let up. Not until the broom handle connected with the battery housing. Then the whole thing came down. All that remained was a gaping hole in the drywall.

Sheetrock dust sullied the air.

Quinn sneezed.

The burning smell had intensified in the melee. He tipped his head back to look at the oven and found dense smoke seeping out around the door.

"The biscuits!" his mom shouted, running to retrieve them.

Adjusting his position, Quinn settled Taylor along the front of his body and tightened his hold. If the woman shook any harder, parts and pieces were going to start falling off her, too.

Without thinking, he stroked a hand up and down her back as he hummed a popular country ballad.

His mom moved into his line of sight, an odd and unfamiliar look on her face. "You had one job, son. One. Job. Stir the gravy. How did *that* turn into *this*?"

A grin pulled at his mouth, the corners tipping up without his consent. He couldn't help it. Honest. "Teach you to run off and leave me in charge of the kitchen."

Her gaze rested on Taylor. "Seriously. What happened?"

"It's personal, her story to tell," he murmured, still stroking the woman's back. "As for what happened here, the smoke alarm went off and she panicked, tried to shut it off and ended up nearly catatonic. The alarm sound triggers her."

His mom didn't hesitate, grabbing the phone and dialing. "I need an ambulance out at the Bradley place." The emergency dispatcher asked a few questions that she answered or asked Quinn to answer, then she listened long enough that he began to get antsy. Then she nodded. "Calm, still, stable. My son will stay with her and I'll drive out to meet the ambulance so they don't miss the turn. Thanks." Disconnecting, she hung the phone up, grabbed her keys and whistled for the dog. "I have my cell. Call me if anything changes."

The quiet in the house pressed against Quinn the second she closed the door behind her. He had emergency medical training, but this thing with Taylor was so much bigger than the categories he was good in, things like "needs stitches" or "brace and immobilize." This injury hid deep, and he didn't have the training to handle it with any kind of expertise. So he did the one thing he could do.

He held her. Talked to her. Rocked her very, very carefully. Told her how amazing she was and more. None of it was enough.

Quinn closed his eyes and thumped his head against the hardwood floor. What was he supposed to do with this?

He and Taylor had only just begun exploring each other, discovering the intimacies inherent to new lovers, talking and laughing less than ten minutes ago. He'd never thought about what had been missing for him emotionally, not until she'd shown up. She'd made him think bigger and want more than he'd ever wanted. Until now. With her, he wanted it all—a house that was a permanent and stationary home, a car payment on a note they signed together, a garden they planted and tended, and a puppy that was representative of future commitments he wasn't brave enough to give a name to.

"Taylor," he said, so softly only she could have heard him.

She sighed and relaxed a fraction more.

He tipped his chin down and frowned. If he hadn't seen her flip out, he wouldn't recognize her now. The haunted fear that had painted her every expression had all but disappeared, so much so that he couldn't help but wonder if, in his own panic, he hadn't perhaps made it more than it had really been.

No. Not him. He'd never been one to embellish anything. He couldn't stand people who did that crap, twisting their recollection of facts to maximize listener investment.

He was going to have to reconsider their climb. She was a potential liability.

But obtaining her recertification means more to her than anything. How can I be the one to prevent her from achieving it? She needs it, needs to know she can do this and be more than the past. If I'm there, I can take extra precautions to keep her safe. I would have done the same for Dad. Maybe this is my chance to make things right.

The idea became all-consuming, that he could make amends for his absence with his dad by seeing Taylor through this while ensuring her safety.

How could he know for sure that this was the right thing, though?

He huffed, the move jostling Taylor.

Her grip on his shirt tightened and her lips opened a bit as she worked through short, panting breaths.

Trailing his fingers up and down her back, he stared at the ceiling. He let his mind wander. The damn thing didn't go far, zooming in on the enigma cradled against his chest. Question after question hit him in rapid-fire succession.

Why does the mind react to memories it couldn't access by achieving a near catatonic state?

What does the smoke alarm represent?

How often did this happen?

His fingers stilled.

What will I do if this happens midclimb?

What do I do if I refuse to climb with her and she goes to someone else?

What if the next guy she hires sucks?

What if he fails to take proper precautions and she gets hurt?

What if she...

His heart stuttered at the thought he couldn't bring himself to complete.

She can't go with anyone else. If I can't talk her out of it, I'll go with her. I'll take every extra precaution I can think of—a revised climb plan, shorten the hours we're on the mountain to the bare minimum, find an easier ascent, map out a hike-able descent. Whatever I have to do. She'll have me by her side to see her through, to ensure she comes out of this alive. I'll do for her what I couldn't do for Dad.

His throat tightened and his eyes burned.

What a difference a couple of hours could make.

Fingers splayed wide, he rested his hand against her lower back.

"Last time you were sprawled across me like this, you were naked," he whispered into her hair. "I like naked better."

A smaller shiver passed through her and he snatched it up and held it close. She'd heard him. He knew it.

So he talked.

Outside, the heavy rumble of an unfamiliar engine, big by the sound of it, fragmented his concentration. Doors slammed. Unfamiliar male voices called back and forth. What sounded like a parade crossed the porch. The door swung open and the dog bounded in ahead of his mother and, behind her, the paramedics, who were in the process of gloving up.

"I can't send them up. It's too dangerous." Taylor was almost seizing against his chest, she twitched so hard. And then, in a heartbreakingly broken voice, she whispered, "No go."

14

Winds were out of the north at thirty-one knots, gusting to forty flat. Wind shear off the mountain's face was sporadic, mild to moderately severe. Conditions were rapidly deteriorating, both above and below the chopper's current altitude. Blowing snow around the mountain's base created near-whiteout conditions, while a late spring storm built above and was forecast to dump up to thirty inches of the white stuff before it blew out. And because Murphy's Law was truly its own religion on the mountain, she had coordinates confirming that the solo climber they'd been sent up to retrieve was on Liberty Ridge, over eight hundred feet above base camp. He couldn't dig in and ride the storm out due to injuries, so rescue was his best, and only, chance at survival.

The bird cleared the tree line, starting the initial approach. And, of course, that's when conditions went from what-was-I-thinking straight to you're-going-to-need-that-vomit-bag-my-friend bad.

The weather reports Taylor had pulled before leaving the rangers' station said it wasn't supposed to be even half this bad, and that wasn't at all good.

Damn it.

Focus softening, Taylor began running the risk analysis through her head, calculating the probability of success based on a variety of factors—weather, the climber's condition, visibility, that capricious bitch people had amusingly named Luck—all stuff she had no control over. Didn't matter. She was the captain, and that made her responsible for her team's well-being, just as they were all responsible for the injured climber's chances of getting out alive. Ultimately, it all came down to her call.

Weather reports were as reliable as the articles in the Hollywood gossip rags. She could garner more firsthand information looking out the window than some guy in front of a computer screen running models ever could. Glancing outside, she caught a tear in the storm's veil. A sliver of clear sky flashed, there then gone. The point wasn't that it disappeared but that it had been there at all. An omen? Maybe. Could also be the storm breaking up. It was impossible to know. Had she seen nothing but mountain, it would have been easy to call it. But it had been sky. Blue sky.

Closing her eyes, she pinched the bridge of her nose. Screw the calculations. This was simple math: six-and-a-pilot go up, seven-and-a-pilot come down.

"*Go or no-go, el capitán?*"

She'd been leaning against the support of the seat harness, but the static-filled voice in her ear startled her into sitting up.

Wind sideswiped the chopper and shoved the bird like the two had a score to settle.

She glanced at the smartphone display, reading dispatch's notes on the climber.

SOS signal received: 17:52
Name: Wilcox, Gary
Gender: Male

Age: 29
Climb Status: Solo
Last Reported Location: Ptarmigan Ridge (NPS Permit MR-147992)
Self-Reported Condition: Lacerations requiring field attention; suspect early-stage hypothermia; possible tib/fib fractures; possible concussion
Action: Mountain Rescue Dispatched
Team: Prime Time
Captain: Taylor Williams
Lieutenant: Tate Anderson

Horizontal sleet pelted the chopper.

The pilot, Monty, cursed as he gave up finessing the stick and manhandled the bastard with brute force.

Lieutenant Tate Anderson, second in command, leaned toward her, shouting to be heard over nature and machine. "Hate to nag, Taylor, but you need to call it." He grinned and winked. "Make us heroes, would ya? Otherwise I'm missing the wife's meat loaf for nothing."

"You're a walking, talking stomach, my friend."

"You've never had her meat loaf. I'll ask her to make it next time you come over. Maybe Friday?"

"Deal."

She slipped her phone into her jacket and then, reaching for her helmet, cued her mic. Static almost blew out her eardrums. She let go of the button, took three deep breaths and tried again. This time, silence.

She hesitated. The storm was bad and there was something...

"Heroes," Tate mouthed and gave her two thumbs-up as he propped one foot on the litter.

"It's a go."

"No…" THE INCOMPLETE command scraped her throat. She tried again. Same results. Hands traced over her skin. Unfamiliar voices spoke in clipped tones that confused her already jumbled thoughts. Medical terminology peppered their conversation.

Why?

A cuff tightened around her biceps at the same time a seriously dense pain shot through the top of her hand.

"Turn her toward me, Justin."

"On three. One, two, three."

She shifted and hands tightened around her as she slipped off…something.

From the fast-receding replay, the sensation of falling rushed her, a shapeless, dark memory she couldn't see, couldn't defend herself from. She curled in on herself and waited, knowing the sound of impact would rip her open and white-hot pain would melt her bones.

Impact.

"No-go!" Taylor shouted, flailing and shoving at the arms that tried to hold her in place. She blinked, her vision so blurry nothing was clear. All she knew was that this wasn't her place or her space. She didn't belong.

An unfamiliar face swam into view. "Calm down, Ms. Williams. We've got you."

"Heart rate is skyrocketing."

Unfamiliar voices went back and forth, talking about her, over her.

"Damn it! I had the IV seated and she pulled it."

"Hand me the gauze. She's bleeding all over the place."

Bleeding.

Anxiety whipped through her, chilling her.

A broad, calloused hand caught hers and held on. "Slow down."

She yanked, trying to free her hand.

The grip tightened. "When you're on the mountain, I'm in control. You *will* listen to me. Got it?"

Another memory, this one auditory, tripped through her consciousness. *Handsome as the devil is dark, and stubborn as a mule to boot, but he's a good man.*

She went lax so fast her head spun.

Strong arms pulled her in close and she smelled familiar skin and comforting heat, felt reassuring strength and understood that there, within those arms, the darkness could never reach her.

Discussion carried on about her but behind her. She didn't hear specifics, didn't want to know what the paramedics wanted to do to her here or where they wanted to take her later. Unless someone surgically excised her from this embrace, she was staying. Laughter rumbled in the chest beneath her ear when she said as much.

"I'm not going to let Justin and his overzealous buddy, Zach, take you in, baby." She relaxed even as the two faceless men protested. "Unless," Quinn said over the melee, "there's a valid reason she needs to go into Clayton or even Amarillo. Then we'll talk to *her* about it."

"I'm not certain she's cognitively aware or stable enough to make decisions about her end-of-life care."

She went completely rigid and forced Quinn to adjust his hold.

"Decisions about her end-of-life care? Seriously, Justin, are you *trying* to push her over the edge?" Quinn all but shouted. "You've got to lay off the Discovery Health channel and afternoon talk TV. You're going to kill someone in your exuberance. I mean, you *do* realize you don't get to perform field autopsies, right?" When the answer was an indignant huff, Quinn lowered his voice. "You go cutting on anything besides your steak at dinner and you and I will have words, Justin. Right before I have fists and you see the dentist."

Taylor breathed, secure in a way she hadn't been since the day of the accident.

More memories.

"See you around, Ms. Bradley."

Elaine's smile could be heard. "Tell your mom I still want to get together to go get raspberries later this summer, Zach."

"Yes, ma'am."

The sound of the stretcher rattling across the floor and down the steps faded, followed by a few parting comments between the paramedics and Elaine. Then the sound of the big diesel engine revved before fading away.

The front door opened and closed before Taylor managed to get her bearings or summon enough bravery to dwarf her embarrassment.

Elaine stopped next to her and Quinn, the smell of cigar smoke and fabric softener an oddly soothing combination. Gently stroking Taylor's head, she spoke to Quinn in a tone that brooked no argument. "Justin needs to get a handle on his enthusiasm for the job or he's going to end up being more of a public menace than he was the summer he heard Reverend Townsend preach on minding your words and your actions so they were in line with one another."

Quinn chuckled and leaned down so his lips were next to Taylor's ear. "Justin was a nosy little shit. He kept asking why this and why that. *Why is Mrs. Ballard married to Mr. Ballard if she's kissing Dr. Youngers?* or *Why does Sheriff Moser's nose bleed after he sniffs car-fist-crated flour power in his nose?*"

Taylor laughed. "You're making that up."

"He's not." Elaine stilled her hand, letting it rest on Taylor's head. "He was trying to ask what 'confiscated' meant in reference to a cocaine bust that made the front page for weeks. My favorite of all, though, was when he went to the front of the church and told the reverend that he'd been doing the Lord's work just like the reverend had asked. The reverend adjusted his tie and smiled, praising Justin for his devout service unto the Lord and then asking him to take his seat. Instead, Justin solemnly folds his hands and says, *I heard Colby's mommy say you were having a baby with her but that it's okay since no one is any wiser. I'm not sure what folks is s'posed to be wiser than, but that's what she said.* Then the kid leans forward, pats the about-to-pass-out reverend on his shoulder and says right into his lapel microphone, *But I don't think you look like you're having a baby. Colby's mom is really big—like she shoved a ball up under her. Maybe two!* First time in the town's little history that the congregation dispersed before the service was delivered."

Humor bubbled up through Taylor and she couldn't help but laugh out loud.

"Welcome back, beautiful," Quinn said, so quietly only she could have heard.

"Thanks for not letting the overzealous paramedic take me away in his meat wagon." She shuddered, only partially for effect.

Quinn stroked her hair and she leaned into the surety of his touch.

The front door opened then closed, and Elaine was gone, leaving them alone.

Driven by timeless instinct, she turned toward the source of comfort. Her heat. Her warmth. Their mouths came together in a move so powerful and sensual it had to have appeared choreographed. This wasn't foreplay. This was a kiss that offered reassurance, the immediate affirmation that this, this was home and you were safe here. A

safe harbor like this was rare if someone was lucky enough
to simply find it in a place, but to find one in a partner? A
partner you could share thoughts and ideas and hopes and
fears and joys and sorrows with? That, right there, was the
height of rare—a once-in-a-lifetime chance.

And Taylor was nobody's fool.

QUINN SPENT EVERY day over the next week putting Taylor
through her paces, and every night loving her body until
they both fell asleep satisfied and with nothing left to give.

Every day started the same, with Quinn doing his
damnedest to get her to give up the climb. From the first
conversation to the most recent one, her responses had
been the same. She intended to make the climb and obtain her recertification to prove to herself she could. Her
last words to him, uttered only yesterday, had closed the
door on any further argument.

"I have to do this, Quinn!" she'd shouted, thumping her
fist over her heart. Her voice had shaken with raw, ragged
emotion. "*Me. I* have to. I need to know that if I don't go
back to the job, it's because I *chose* not to, not that fear
rendered me incapable. I need to know that it's my choice
to walk away. Don't you get it?"

"I don't want you taking the chance, Taylor." Quinn had
moved in, framing her face with his broad, work-roughened
hands. "Make the choice to walk away now. Make the choice
to let this go, to let it be finished now. Today. That can be
your choice."

She'd gripped his wrists and stared at him, her hazel
eyes darkened with emotion. "That's not the choice I could
ever make and live with. If you know me at all, you know
this isn't about winning or being the best or proving a
point to anyone else. This is about me laying my past to
rest and moving on." She'd sighed and closed her eyes be-

fore dropping the hammer on him. "What would you do, what wouldn't you give, to know that your presence that day at the windmill wouldn't have changed anything?"

"Look at me," he'd demanded, waiting until she did. "The difference is that your recertification *doesn't* change anything, Taylor. You weren't in charge of the chopper that went down. You weren't responsible for the accident."

"I made the damn call!" She'd shaken head to toe. "All I can do is tell you that, somehow, doing this allows me to close the door to that part of my life on my terms. It's all I've got, Quinn, and it has to be enough." Her chin had quivered but she'd borne down on the surge of emotion, riding it out until it passed and she was able to whisper the last. "Help me see it through. Please. Don't take this from me. I have to confront this head-on. Otherwise? I'll spend the rest of my life waiting for the next thing that triggers me, wondering how to live half a life and pretend it's enough."

Her plea had done him in, and he hadn't been able to deny her because she'd been spot-on in so many ways, but one in particular. There was nothing he wouldn't do to find a way, any way, to close the door on the deep-seated terror that he hadn't been the son he should have been. If he could do this for her, maybe, just maybe, he'd be lucky enough to find a way to forgive himself for failing his dad.

Going forward, he made it a point each day to train her harder than the day before, pushing her right up to the edge of her limits as she saw them and then beyond. He created new limits, new boundaries, as he pulled every trick from his bag to ensure she was ready for anything the mountain might throw at them. She also needed to be ready to work through any memories that climbing might trigger.

But so did he.

That had become more than apparent the first time he'd

strapped her into her all-new gear and sent her up a simple rope via her harness and a pair of ascension grips. She made it roughly twelve feet up before the sweats hit her. Next came shaking. Then tears. She moved on to attempting to negotiate with him. When that didn't work, she found imaginary fault with the gear. Then came the argumentative stage.

That phase took a while.

She rounded things out with threats to his person, with claiming to need to use the restroom, and finally with acceptance. She climbed the remaining ten feet to ring the bell and let herself down. It wasn't until she had her feet on the ground that he'd pointed out she could have taken that option at any point. There had been a few words that were, well, *hostile* wasn't a strong enough description.

And the first time he put her on what she'd dubbed the K-12—*"Tell me you've seen the movie* Better Off Dead. *No? You're dead to me."*—he'd been left wondering if this incredible thing that continued to grow, this connection they'd found with each other, was already at its end after she professed to hate him. What she felt for his climbing machine was far stronger than mere hate.

Now, with her unhooking from the K-12, he looked her over carefully. "Nice form, Williams."

"You talking about my ass or my dismount?" she asked as she released the last of her carabiners and quick draws, and reattached them to her harness. "Because both are fabulous."

He moved in behind her and settled his hands on her waist. "Why does it have to be one or the other? Because you're right. Both are pretty damn spectacular."

"I'm paying you for your professional instruction, not your opinion on the appearance of my backside when it's literally in a sling."

"That observation's free, sweetheart." A gentle slap to the referenced cheek and she was suddenly facing him, her lips on his, their breath commingled, her hands as greedy as his and her need for him as untempered as his for her.

Adjusting his position, he lifted her. "Legs around my waist."

She complied, but not before she issued a command of her own. "Don't bother with the cottage. Too far and I don't want to wait."

Their mouths engaged in a near battle with each other, each seeking to gain the upper hand, lay claim to the body's territory and conquer the opposing side without mercy or reprieve.

As if she'd read his mind, she broke the kiss, her ragged breath making her sound all the more like a seductress. "Consider me the spoils of your war on my terror."

He grinned. "You know, that works for me."

"Don't think, Monroe. Do."

The very words he'd thrown at her all week when she'd frozen up. How appropriate she got to lob them back at him after she'd mastered the machine that most terrified her. "Doing, Williams. Trust me." He hesitated a brief second, wondering if she'd notice his slip. Those two words, issued right here less than two weeks ago, had pushed them to this point. Her reaction then had been to shut him down and try to shut him out. He didn't know what would happen if—

"I do."

He froze. "Excuse me?"

She brushed her lips over his in the most tender of kisses. "I do trust you."

There was sudden awareness of something foreign inside him. It, this *thing*, shifted around, expanding to fill every available nook and cranny, and some that couldn't be deemed "easily accessible." The thing pushed anyway, and its unfamiliar breadth and girth left him struggling for air even as it squeezed his heart. The sensation stopped as suddenly as it had begun. It didn't go away but seemed to settle in for the duration.

What the hell was that?

No time to mess with it now. He had a hot, willing, wonderful woman in his arms, and she demanded his full attention. And she trusted him to make sure she got it.

Quinn wasn't about to let her down.

Tightening his hold on her, he thrilled at her little noise of anticipation. Several steps forward and he had her back pressed to the broad beam of the climbing machine she so hated. Why not give her a good memory? He'd make this woman come apart in his arms, and he'd do it here. Whatever it took.

"Arms above your head and grip the beam. Don't let go. Hear me?"

She complied and then arched her back, pressing her breasts upward and groaning when he gave each a little nip through her shirt.

He propped her sex against his thigh and, with deft movements, stripped her to nothing. To keep her skin from getting pinched, he wedged her T-shirt between her back and the metal beam she rested against. That was all the nicety he had left in him.

He had a split second to wonder if his eyes were as wild as hers before he caught their reflection in her depths. Answer that one in the affirmative. He looked like a wild man. A crazed man. A man in love.

Quinn's body reacted with a violent, head-to-toe muscle spasm and he nearly dropped her. Taylor. The woman he…loved.

Love. I love her. I'm in love *with Taylor Williams.*

No matter how he phrased it, the declaration sounded right.

That huge, foreign creature inside him settled deeper into place. Oddly, it fit as if entity and space had been made for each other and had just been waiting for the proper introduction.

So that's what love feels like.

"Don't stop," she pleaded, moving against him.

Loving you? Never. I can't. You're mine. How do I tell you you're mine?

He opened his mouth to tell her what he'd realized, to say those three words burning a hole in his chest, but nothing happened. Everything was so tangled up inside that he couldn't separate it and put the right pieces in motion. This stuff needed to come with an instruction manual and some kind of video. Since it didn't, he'd simply show her what he didn't know how to say.

Reaching between them, he fumbled with his jeans, working them down his thighs with more force than finesse. The end result was the same. Once freed, his cock jutted from his body with determined force. He pulled out a condom, but Taylor snagged it, ripping it open and rolling it down his length in one fluid motion.

She looked up and grinned. "You're taking too long."

He grinned…and pulled her down his length at the same time he pushed up and into her hot, wet sheath.

She cried out, widening her thighs and pushing down on him, taking him all the way to the hilt.

Quinn spread his feet wider, gripped her hips and leaned back. "Look at me, Taylor." He waited a split second for her passion-glazed gaze to find his. "See me." The words were as much a plea as they were a command. Trusting she would understand, he went from stationary to a driving force, thrusting into her with long, strong, solid strokes that rocked her lithe body.

She let go of the metal beam behind her, clinging, instead, to him. Hands that had earned every scar and callus, hands he'd grown to admire as well as covet, grabbed his neck and used it as a fulcrum from which she levered her body up and over his rigid shaft. Tiny sounds of encouragement and larger sounds of need sneaked out of her, and he doubted she was even aware. Not with the way her stare bored into his.

"Quinn." His name on her lips was soft, an invocation he didn't deserve but claimed.

She was his.

Their joining took on a whole new meaning that cemented in place the emotions he'd finally been able, or brave enough, to give definition.

Sharp pleasure spread along his spine and through his sac, the latter drawing up tight. She had to go over the edge first. He'd follow. Always. But she was first in everything. Now and always.

He leaned back farther and used his hips for more support, more leverage. Then he reached between them, found her clit and worked her over the way he knew she liked.

Her core fluttered once, twice, then tightened, seizing around him with incredible strength. Taylor gripped handfuls of his shirt and bit her bottom lip, threw her head back and rode out the orgasm.

She was so. Damn. Beautiful.

Quinn's release was building one moment and taking him apart the next. His vision shattered so that he saw Taylor in a thousand prisms, her skin flushed, eyes bright, hair falling down. She was his everything, and he didn't know how to say it, to get it right, so that she might believe him. Until he figured it out and could do the moment justice, he'd sit on the knowledge and work harder to show her exactly what she meant to him every moment of every day.

Resting his forehead against hers, he met her gaze, willing her to see in his eyes the words he couldn't quite say.

I love you.

15

"DIDN'T THE WEATHER report say temperatures would be above average?" Taylor absently clicked the carabiner she held—open-closed, open-closed—as she suppressed a hard shiver. The wind had more than a bite to it. The gusts were freezing her bone marrow. "This can't be average."

"Your hands are cold, muscles are tight and heart rate is high. I bet you're also sweating and a little nauseous." Quinn peered up the first leg—a short but scrambling ascent Taylor couldn't stop staring at. "How close am I?"

She made a sound of disgust punctuated with a sharp glare. "Close enough."

"I'm spot-on and you know it."

"If it's that important to you, give up the glory and get a desk job with a map maker," she said, but there was no bite to her bark.

Less than fourteen hours ago, she'd been coming off a sexual high so steep she'd almost needed supplemental oxygen. Eyes closed, limbs limp to the point of uselessness, she had asked for a piece of paper and a pen.

"Why?" Quinn's skepticism had been evident.

"I've found my happy place. I need to bookmark it so I can always find my way back."

He'd been silent for several seconds. Then he'd leaned in and whispered, "I won't ever let you get that lost." Then he'd set her down on wobbly legs—His? Hers? Theirs?—and, pants around his knees, chose that moment of sexual torpor to yank the rug out from under her. "Your form is spot on. Your decisions are grounded in common sense and based on thinking through not just your next move but your next four to six moves. Your approach to problem-solving in harness is more than I hope for from most students."

He tilted his chin back and stared at the ceiling, his next words as softly spoken as they were rough around the edges. "Your argument about why you need to do this is something I can't refute and won't deny you, no more than I expect you to cut me out and deny my need to be there to see you through. Get your gear together and do the preclimb safety check, then pack it up. We'll leave for the park in two hours and make camp before dark. Your re-cert climb starts tomorrow morning at Trono del Cielo."

She'd stumbled through a response, her lips numb and her chest tighter than a corporal's sheets during military bed check. "What? Why tomorrow? When did you decide to go? How can you expect me to be prepared without warning? Where are we going again?" Heart in her throat, she'd grabbed his face and kissed him hard. "You won't regret this. I know I'm ready. I can do this, Quinn. I have to do this. Thank you. Thank you a million times over."

He had looked at her long and hard before responding. "If I didn't truly believe in you, this climb wouldn't happen. You can do this, Taylor. Everything you've done has convinced me you are absolutely capable." He pressed his forehead to hers and closed his eyes. "Everything you've said has convinced me that you absolutely need to. But we go together. You will listen to me up there as your instructor, not your lover. Got it?" He'd opened his eyes and stared at her long and hard. "Your word, Taylor."

"I swear to you I will do what you tell me to do and go where you tell me to go."

He'd nodded and stepped away, put himself to rights and stalked out of the barn, calling over his shoulder, "My truck in two hours."

Now, standing at the first ascent, a steep incline of loose rock that had, over time, fallen off the mountain, she couldn't stop her toes from curling in her hiking shoes. Known as a scree field, the shifting rock made walking a certifiable sport, complete with wounds, injuries, accidents and, on occasion, casualties.

She choked on her inhale.

Not going there.

No way had she geared up like Wilma the Mountain Wonder to punk out. That didn't stop her mind from throwing options at her. The best yet was to run screaming, get as far away as possible and enroll in coursework to become a certified pastry chef. She'd heard France had good cooking schools, and that was just about far enough away.

But she would spend the rest of her life wondering what might have happened if she'd done what needed to be done, obtained her recertification in specialized mountain search and rescue, and returned to work.

I'm not cut out for long-term what-ifs.

"So nut up or shut up," she murmured to herself, taking her first step onto the scree field.

Quinn was by her side in a heartbeat, taking her arm and pointing toward a narrow path. "Trono del Cielo has a moderately passable if ridiculously narrow path across the lower scree. Think of it as walking a tightrope made of shale over a shale safety net that hovers over a shale lake.

And watch for any loose shale on the tightrope. It'll set you on your ass and send you on your way in nothing flat."

"Sounds lovely." She gestured toward the mountain. "And when we reach the other side?"

"We discover which came first—chicken or egg." He laughed as he tucked a loose curl behind her ear. "Kidding. After we come off the scree field, we'll make the ascent to the major climb field. We'll go up most of the way, camp on the ascent, summit early tomorrow morning and begin the descent immediately. Should be back to the car tomorrow evening. We'll either stay one more night or head back to the ranch."

"How long before my recertification paperwork clears?" she asked.

"Shouldn't take long."

The tenor of his answer struck her as off, but he turned away before she could search his face for truth. They'd have to deal with whatever it was later. Right now, she had the Scree-Shale Field from Hell to cross and a mountain to climb and memories to recover. Or not. Just depended on what the universe deemed luck versus retribution.

Too often they looked eerily similar.

FOUR HOURS AND one short memory reveal later, they'd made it to the launch site for the climb. She'd suffered little more than a scraped palm and mildly bruised knee—stupid slate was slicker than ice—and an insignificant strained muscle. The latter was both the mildest and largest of her concerns, because it created an identifiable weakness that miscalculation could exploit.

The memory had been a split-second recollection of the sound of the wind. She'd managed to keep hold of the present by the very skin of her fingertips, shrugging the memory off before Quinn could question her.

None of it, individually or collectively, would be enough to stop her. It may have taken her a while to understand that she needed to do this so she could stop looking back and start looking forward, but the point was that she'd made the connection. She owed Quinn for all of it. If it hadn't been for his help, guidance and unfailing faith in her, she would have caved. Now? She was ready to let the past lie. She only needed this last piece so she could close that chapter of her life.

Staring up the lee, the side of the mountain protected from the wind, she calculated snowfields and rock climbs and exposed ground. The snow speckled the mountain in varying concentrations and depths, small and large pockets glistening behind and between boulders. Thin ice sheeted the deepest deposits, while those shallow snowbanks more prone to a higher concentration of melt and refreeze had more substantial sheeting. When the elements were combined with the variable pitch, she realized it was the perfect climb to determine a person's advanced skill and decision-making capabilities.

Memories of her team's traditions and the wacky superstitions they'd held dear were impossible to ignore. On their last mission, Tate had taped their mascot, a little vending-machine troll named Commodore, to the front of his helmet and promised a full report via Troll Vision, postrescue. The man was off-center enough that his "troll talk" had been reliably hysterical and regularly requested.

She'd brought the beer and Fig Newtons for postflight celebrations.

Her pilot, Monty—

A warm hand settled at the nape of her neck, and she nearly went ninja on the poor soul. Of course it was Quinn. Who else would it be?

Ghosts. Memories.

He squeezed her neck gently as if he understood her thoughts and where they'd gone. "I want to get going so there's plenty of time to establish camp."

Taylor nodded, eyeing the climb ahead of her. No. Ahead of *them*. She wasn't alone in this.

"Pretty straightforward climb for a Grade IV."

They were getting ready to go up, to retrieve the solo climber. Weather was moving in, but it didn't look like it would be too bad and she said as much.

"Nothing's ever what it seems on the mountain, captain." Tate tapped the green troll on his helmet. "Commodore knows."

She knew better. Truly, she did. She *knew* she wasn't talking to Tate. That didn't stop her from taking a stiff-legged step forward, out of Quinn's reach, and then stumbling around to look for the man she had loved, and now missed, like a brother.

"Taylor?" Quinn didn't crowd her, but he stayed within reach.

A cloud rolled over the sun, casting an unnatural shadow over the noon hour.

Go or no-go, captain?

"First step is always the hardest, baby, but technically? You've already taken it." Quinn's warm presence closed in. "That makes this something like the five-thousandth step, and we all know it's hella-easier at this point than it was down there. Worst part of all will be the meal kits." His lips caressed the shell of her ear. "This is your time and your climb, Williams. *You. Own. It.*"

She felt a huge weight slip away and breathing became easier. Making the call to go up or go home wasn't her responsibility, not now, not for this climb. No one's life was in her hands. No one was depending on her to see them up or down the mountain safely or to safety. Quinn wasn't counting on her to do anything but climb so he could do his job and document her skill sets—the same ones he'd spent the last week and a half affirming before he'd take her up. He'd made it clear in their internet correspondence that if she didn't satisfactorily pass the ground work, he wouldn't approve her to make the climb. Obviously, she'd passed his inspection as well as his brutal training plan.

He believed in her.

What lay in front of her now was the chance to reclaim the faith she'd lost in herself. She wasn't facing this alone, though. He was here and would be here, with her, the whole time, ready and willing to assist should she stumble.

She didn't plan on needing him for more than companionship and victory sex.

"Let's do this thing."

QUINN HAD WATCHED Taylor make a clinically perfect climb. Twice she'd stopped and had to fight off a wave of fear or a dark memory. Whatever the episodes had been, he hadn't asked, had simply expected her to push through, and she had.

They were roughly halfway up the primary face, preparing to switch up their approach to compensate for the change in terrain, when a sudden gust of wind hit. No, not *hit*. It was an invisible sucker punch that ripped him off the face of the rock. He fell, the sickening free fall driving his nuts into his liver. He hit the last safety anchor he'd driven into the rock, his body flexing to its limit. The anchor held, thank God.

Momentum sent him spinning out into space, nothing above him but darkening sky, nothing below but a landing he'd only make once. Regaining control of the spin was a bare-fisted alley brawl as he tried to counter the motion, anticipate his next point of contact and find a sufficient grip or toehold to at least slow him down. No luck. Each bounce jarred him, rattling him like a piece of candy in a piñata, until the whole thing became an exercise in minimizing physical damage.

Sunlight gave way to shadow as clouds raced across the sky. He alternated between being suspended on the rope and donating skin to the mountain when he made skipping contact with the granite face. Then he *really* hit, hard enough he didn't bounce back. His shoulder protested the angle of abuse as momentum wedged him into a crevice between a tall, slender boulder and the sheer face. Not a good place to be. He wasn't in trouble, exactly, but close enough to it to pick out defining traits. Never good.

"Hang tight, Taylor," he shouted against the gusting wind. "It's all good, baby. Give me a minute to get sorted and I'll be right there."

Closest he'd come to lying in ages, and, of course, it had to be with her.

The day just kept getting better.

Light broke through the clouds and drew his attention skyward. Earlier, the sky had been a brilliant blue with sporadic cloud cover. That had changed in the last half hour. Clouds had pulled together, growing dense and dark as a storm that hadn't been forecast brewed. Daylight gave way to unnatural dusk. The smell of rain permeated his senses.

Quinn rested his forehead against the boulder that pinned him. His stomach was in knots, only a few of which could be attributed to using his body in an unplanned game of hopscotch across the mountain's north face. The majority of his concern was for Taylor. This—his fall, the weather, being forced to make critical decisions on the mountain—any of this could trigger her, and then what? How would he get her off the mountain if she was catatonic? He'd been so convinced he could control the outcome, could intercept any potential catastrophe simply by being present and aware, that he'd ended up putting her in the worst possible position. This was on him and him alone.

God save him, he'd been such a fool.

The only thing he could do was stay close while keeping her engaged and moving. That meant freeing his shoulder and working through the pain and possible injury. It would be easier if his arm wasn't wedged into the narrow space like a french fry dropped between the console and the front seat.

He struggled to free his shoulder, pulling, wiggling, issuing threats and damning the mountain straight to hell. Nothing worked. Quinn sagged against the mountain's hold, sweat dripping into his eyes and his muscles quivering with exhaustion.

Then Taylor was there. Eyes wide, she panted instead of breathing. Fear slicked her skin so it gleamed, even in the dim light. The corner of one eye twitched sporadically. None of that mattered. She had crossed the face on her own and she was there.

She looked him over and her lips twitched.

He was prepared for tears, panic, sharp words…but that wasn't what came out of her mouth.

"That was both the best and the worst Tarzan impersonation I've ever seen."

"Shut up, Jane."

She laughed, the sound rich and vibrant, and only slightly underscored with hysteria.

"How are you, Taylor?"

Throat working as she swallowed, she responded with a shallow nod and two simple words that spoke volumes. "I'll do."

He dipped his chin and caught her gaze. "I'll get us out of this." Another promise that had the potential to be a lie. He was on a roll.

"How about *we* get us out of this? Believe it or not, I have a little experience with this search-and-rescue stuff." She rubbed her hands together before rapping her knuckles on the top of his pack. "Tell me you packed some cooking spray in here, darling. I'll slick you up and have you out of here in no time."

He shot her a deadpan look before he began working again to free his shoulder. Like before, nothing he did—yanking, tugging, cursing, pulling—made any difference. Intent on gaining leverage, he made a fist with the hand on his pinned arm and frowned. The movement was no longer easy and the hand had begun to tingle.

A bitter shot of panic left a foul taste at the back of his tongue and surprised a short gasp out of him. *Calm. Just...stay calm.*

Or not. He wrenched his shoulder with as much strength as he could muster, not ashamed to rely on brute force and foul language to get the job done. The result was zero total movement but a hell of a lot of pinched skin, pulled muscles and the sensation of his shoulder joint separating. That last was more than a little discomfort that bordered on pain. It flat-ass *hurt*.

The joint popped and sent fierce agony drilling through the ends of his fingertips, and flashing and pulsing up his neck to his ear. A shout gathered in his chest and then sank down, only to launch itself up and out with brutal force. The sound went on and on until his throat was raw and his oxygen spent. Chin dipping to chest, he hung there under the weight of something akin to desperation...but bigger. Much, much bigger.

Lightning split the sky and the resulting thunder was

instantaneous, its *crack–boom* reverberating through the mountain and, consequently, him.

Taylor clung to the rock beside him, her eyes wide.

"Hang in there, Taylor."

She didn't respond.

Oh, hell.

"Taylor, talk to me."

Still no response.

Reality arrived with little pomp and no circumstance. With Quinn pinned like he was and losing all feeling and function in that arm, the odds of the two of them making it off this mountain dropped by the second. And when he added in Taylor's burgeoning catatonic state, the odds didn't drop. They plummeted.

So Quinn began to talk. Anything and everything he could think of that might get her to come back to herself, to him. He told her about growing up and feeling trapped in the smallest possible fraction of a huge world that had so much to see and do and experience. He told her how much he'd always wanted his dad to adopt him and make him a Bradley, to take away the feeling of illegitimacy that his biological father's last name left him with.

He told her what it was like to get the call that his dad had died and to carry around this unbearable burden that, just maybe, if Quinn had been there, if he'd stayed and worked the ranch, maybe he could've saved his dad's life. He told her how much he missed his dad, that it was a pulsing ache that never went away. He told her about the fear of losing everything his dad had worked for, about the nagging anxiety that he didn't have the ability to supplement the ranch's income, and he didn't know what to do to save his mom.

And he told her about finding out his mom was sleeping with Sam, the area vet, and how it had messed him up, and now he was here and he'd left things wrong between them and he needed to see his mom again to make things right because all he wanted was for her to be happy.

And, with nothing left, he told her the thing he most wanted her to know.

"Then you showed up, a woman with a man's name and the inaugural renter of the cottage-slash-cabin on my family's ranch to boot. I thought I was ready for you, Taylor—that I could *manage* you and get paid to do it. Then I'd send you on your way and have a chunk of change in my pocket to prove I'd *handled you* right." He laughed, the sound bitter and hard. "I was an absolute fool."

Quinn tried to anchor his heels and push up, desperate to relieve some of the pressure on his shoulder and arm. It helped for a few seconds but he couldn't sustain it. The pain was worse when he eased himself back down. His lungs ached with every breath as his chest bore the pressure of hanging unsupported. This wasn't how he'd imagined this, wasn't what he'd wanted. "We're out of time."

A volley of emotions hammered him, but it was, at least initially, joy when Taylor turned toward him. He didn't even consider the strange look on her face.

"Say that again," she croaked.

"We're out of time?"

Rage blanketed her features and left him so confused he wasn't at all concerned he'd poured his heart out to her and she'd only managed to be pissed off. He didn't understand why her neck corded and her nostrils flared, or why the skin bunched around her eyes and her lips flattened.

"Before that."

"I'm not sure—"

"The part where you said you thought you'd manage me and get paid to do it. That part." She asked, tone flat, "I heard that right, didn't I?"

"It wasn't the whole thought, just part of it." He shook the rain out of his face and his shoulder screamed in protest, dragging from him an involuntary shout of pain. "I didn't mean it. Not like that." He knew he was flubbing the conversation, but agony muddled his thoughts and made him slow. Thoughts jumbled and his vision blurred, but he could see well enough to see raw grief etch lines in Taylor's face that were so deep he thought they'd almost have to be permanent. "Taylor?"

"Shut up. Shut up. Shut up, shut up, shut up!" she shouted. "You're no better than my father, treating me like a trainable tool, using me when it's convenient and tucking me away when it's not. I was such a fool!" She slapped a palm against the granite before resting her head beside it.

He saw her lips move but couldn't hear her over the storm. "Taylor," he snapped. "You listen to me."

She pivoted to face him, her eyes flat and lifeless. "I'm done listening to you. I thought… I thought…" Tipping her face to the rain, she laughed, the sound as grating as it was heartbreaking.

"What?" he called, half desperate and half pissed off. "Talk to me."

"No can do, cowboy. Turns out that, of the two of you, I should have listened to my dear old dad, because he was right." She swallowed so hard he saw the muscles in her throat work. "Never divide your attentions. Focus on one thing as your primary life goal. If you divide your attention and give half to one endeavor and half to another, you can only expect fifty-percent returns on each venture." She dug through her pack and retrieved her SAT phone. "At least he was honest with me, Quinn. He never pretended to love me."

"I didn't pretend," he snarled.

"My bad," she said, voice broken, powering up the

phone and then hitting the red emergency beacon button. The phone responded with a sharp beep, sending out an SOS even as it began to dial for emergency help.

"Taylor, you listen to me and you listen now. I love—"

"Don't!" she shouted. "Don't you *dare* take this there."

A disembodied voice squawked over the speaker.

She held up a single finger as if she were on a social call but her words were sharp and delivered with brutal efficiency. "This is Taylor Williams. My climbing partner, Quinn Monroe, and I are on the leeward side of Trono del Cielo. Weather's tanked. My partner has sustained significant injuries, including—"

Quinn listened to her rattle off accurate, concise information. Sounded like they stood a very good chance of making it out of this, after all.

Thanks to her.

She'd done what she needed to do to heal and had saved herself, and him, in the process. He was beyond proud of her.

"Rescue will be here within fifteen minutes. Turns out we weren't the only people on the mountain who required retrieval." She looked at him and smiled, but the gesture never reached her eyes. "Who'd have thought I'd count myself lucky?"

There were a hundred things he wanted to say to her but only one that mattered. Using the last of his strength, he pushed up with his feet and tried to steal enough breath to shout, to force her to hear him over the storm. All he ended up getting was a mouthful of rainwater.

"Save your strength," she called, beginning the process of tying off ropes to create as safe a recovery opportunity as possible. "You're going to need it for recovery. Trust me when I tell you it's a real bitch."

Anything else he might have said was lost to the sound

of chopper blades rising up through the cloud cover and growing louder by the second. The cavalry was near, but they wouldn't make it in time to resuscitate the one thing he most wanted to save.

The love of the woman he'd never seen coming.

16

QUINN STARED AT THE acoustic ceiling tiles and counted them for what had to be the millionth time.

Twenty-two across, twelve deep.

The hospital room was pretty decent in size and had a lovely view of the industrial-sized air-conditioning units on the roof two stories down. A sliver of blue sky could be seen between the neighboring high-rises.

Quinn closed his eyes as the door creaked open.

"He's sleeping, Elaine. We can come back later after he's had some rest."

"Sleeping my fanny," his mother responded, calm and cool. "I saw you through the window before we came in. Stop playing around."

He didn't move, praying she and Sam would move on and leave him be.

The air stirred and the familiar scent of his mother's perfume tickled his nose. "Now you listen to me, young man. I am *not* going to the courthouse to get married without talking to you first."

Quinn sputtered and dove straight to personal protest before his eyes were fully open. "Wha—? No. Just, no. You need to slow your roll, Mom. You're not marrying Sam.

You two haven't been seeing each other long enough to know if it would work or not."

She grinned at him. "Well, look who's awake."

Sam stood in the background, high color riding a pale face. It was the damnedest combination. The vet waved at Quinn, pointed to his ring finger and shook his head.

Quinn shifted his glare to his mom. "Underhanded tactics. You're dealing with an injured man here."

She braced her hands on the bed's side rail and leaned forward. "Yes, I am. Did you know that I asked the nurse if you'd had anything for pain?"

He glanced at Sam, who nodded in affirmation and then stared at the ceiling.

"What did the nurse say?" Dangerous question, but Quinn wanted to know.

"She said yes. Naturally, I asked what you'd been given. She said you'd had Demerol. I told her that was lovely, but I was more interested in them treating your long-standing pain condition." She leaned closer. "Because you're a certifiable *PITA—pain in the ass*. Apparently she's dealt with you enough to have experienced your crappy attitude. She didn't bat an eye when she offered me your next pain management dose."

Quinn couldn't help it. He laughed. "Well played, Mom."

She pulled up a chair, folded her arms on the bed rail and rested her chin on her wrist. "They say you're out in three more days."

"Same thing they told me." He looked out the window again.

"You coming home?" she asked softly.

He closed his eyes and let his head fall back onto the pillow. "I don't have anywhere else to go."

"You can always come home." She stroked his hair off his forehead. "Sam, would you give us a minute?"

"You bet, darlin'. I'll go see if I can't find a priest or minister in-house who might be willing to oversee our vows. I saw cake in the cafeteria line and they'd just filled the sweet-tea jug, so the reception's covered."

"Not helping," Quinn groused.

"Not trying to," Sam quipped, his smile evident.

The door opened quietly and then closed, the latch loud in the hospital's silence.

"How are you really doing, Quinn?"

He'd known the question was coming. It had only been a matter of time. That didn't mean he had a half-decent answer, though. Far from it. Instead of throwing out empty words she'd see right through, he lifted his one good shoulder in a half-hearted shrug. "I'm alive. That's apparently supposed to count for something."

"It is."

Her solemn answer shamed him. "That wasn't fair, Mom. Sorry."

She made a sound of acknowledgement, and then they sat in silence. There was comfort in having her here, but it wasn't her comfort he craved like an addict on his second day of detox.

The soft, warm skin of his mom's hand rested against his cheek and stubbled jaw. "I don't know exactly what you're going through, but I can tell you I felt the same way—that I should count being alive a blessing—after your dad died. I…" She cleared her throat. "I wasn't grateful, Quinn. Not even with you there, though your presence in the house kept me from falling apart at the seams. Taking care of my son? Well, that gave me purpose when all I wanted to do was curl up, pull the covers over my head and figure out how a broken heart could possibly keep me alive."

That. So much that.

She understood. And that she did? He choked on the rush of emotions he'd kept beaten back. Barely, but he'd done it. It took two tries to ask the question he most needed the answer to. "What do I do, Mom? I love her. I love her more than anything, and I botched it up so royally she didn't just leave me, she left the region."

"What did you do to botch it up?" The quiet question held no judgment, but rather a need for understanding founded on a whole lot of love.

So he told her. All of it. From the moment he'd met Taylor at the mercantile to the last he'd seen of her when she'd helped the local search-and-rescue team pull the litter he'd been on into the chopper. "She left without a word the minute we touched down."

Gripping his good hand, the woman who knew him better than any other laid it out in a way only she could. "Quinn, listen to me. You love her, and she knows that. She does," she asserted when he started to protest. "But you treated the chance at forever with her as something with a shelf life, something that ran the risk of expiring before you were good and ready to make a commitment. You don't look for love in the quick-sale bin, darling boy, because forever has no expiration date."

He shot her a bland look.

"Did you or did you not tell her you loved her for the very first time right before you were afraid you were going to meet your Maker?"

"That's just it. I didn't exactly tell her how I felt. Feel," he amended. At her incredulous look, he added, "She never gave me the chance."

"Quinn, you cannot hold her actions against her when you never said to her what most needed to be said…what she most needed to hear."

The sigh that escaped him was answer enough.

"You didn't offer her anything but heartache. You gave her the time she'd paid for and expected her gratitude. Her father did the same to her from the sounds of it—expected her to be indebted to him for any time he bestowed upon her. No woman worth her salt takes that from a man when she's old enough to make the choice for herself."

"I'd rather be loved like that for a few minutes than never," he countered, voice low and raw.

"No, son, you wouldn't. Trust me. You will always want one more hour, even a minute, but you'd settle for a single second just to have that one more time, and it's never enough."

"I screwed up so bad," he mumbled, propping the crook of his good arm over his forehead. "I don't know how to make this right, but I have to." His eyes burned and his throat went tight. "I don't know what to do, Mom. How do I make this right and still be the son Dad would've expected me to be? I can't go after her with the stipulation that, if she loves me, it has to be here versus Washington. And I won't leave you to manage the ranch on your own."

She sighed. "Quinn, sometimes you have to stop doing what everyone else thinks you should do or need to do or are obligated to do, and instead, you do what's right for *you*. You stop listening to the bitchy old women whispering behind your back while you cash out at the grocery line. You stop wondering if the bank vice president, who you turned down twice before getting involved with anyone, is going to deny your loan application because you didn't drop your jeans and wag your drooping white ass when his *married* but esteemed self beckoned. Sometimes you have to face off with life and flip it the bird and tell it to take its best shot because you're not going to roll over and die.

"You hear me, and you hear me loud and clear, son. I've been where you are. I loved your father with every cell of my being. A part of me died when he died. A big part. And I thought, that's it, Elaine. You're alone. You're too young and it's too early, but here you are. You're going to end up living your life out here and dying and it'll be forty-eight days before anyone finds your body, probably in your T-shirt and granny panties, standing at the sink where your heart stopped." She stopped and gulped in a huge breath and pressed on. "I think about these things, Quinn, and I'm scared. But it can't stop me from doing what's right for *me*."

"And that would be Sam? Don't sleep with the vet because you're scared, Mom."

"Son, you did *not* just imply I'm whoring my body out to have my emotions soothed."

The death threat in her voice made him cringe and hang his head. "No, ma'am."

"Damn right you didn't."

"While the sentiment of chasing love down and holding on tight appeals, it doesn't solve the issue of the ranch." He rubbed his forehead with his good hand. "I can't walk away from it. It's my home, my place and my legacy. I want to make it work."

"I'm open to suggestions," she said quietly. "You're going to inherit it someday. I'm of a mind to turn it over to you in deed, as well as name, so this is a decision that's going to impact you the most over the coming years."

He nodded, fussing with the edge of the sheet. "We have options, most of which we never talked about for one reason or the other."

"I think we were both so busy grieving your dad that we failed at that more than once."

Quinn rolled his good shoulder and nodded. "I've been thinking about the size of the place. It's more than we can manage together. If we were to downsize by subleasing some of the Bureau of Land Management pastureland, we could cover about half of the expenses on the main ranch, particularly those related to regular upkeep. It would also give us a small source of annual income, relieving us of the necessity of renewing our operating loan every year. It's not ideal, I know, but I really think we could make this work. Jim Jameson to the north of us would be my first choice. He's bought up everything for sale around him for thirty-plus years, so maybe he'd be open to a lease. The plat says there's a solid three thousand acres between us. We could lease that and see how it works. We could even offer him a one- or three-year lease to ensure it works for all of us."

Her face shone with hope for the first time since he'd been home, and the knots of worry and anxiety lodged in Quinn's chest unraveled. "That's brilliant, Quinn. It's worth talking to Jim. Do you want me to approach him or do you want to do it?"

Quinn didn't miss a beat. "I need to do this, Mom. Dad was counting on me to cowboy up should the need present itself. He wanted me to come home, which I did. He would have wanted me to see you taken care of, which I'm going to do. And he would have wanted me to keep as much of the ranch in the family as possible, which I will. Leasing some of the land will get us some cash flow and help us get ahead financially. When we're back on solid ground, we can talk about how to take back control of the whole place."

"Your dad would be proud," Elaine said quietly.

"I hope so. I'm doing the best I know to do and still keep the ranch in the family. Selling off isn't an option he would have wanted us to explore unless every other option had been exhausted." He shifted his focus to settling his covers just so before summoning the courage to face her on a different topic altogether. "I want you to be happy,

Mom, and I know Dad absolutely never wanted anything less. If Sam makes you happy, I'm going to shut up about it other than to say this. I love you and wish you all the happiness you can grab."

Her eyes shone with unshed emotion. "I'm lonely, Quinn, and I miss your dad. I will always miss him. Just like Sam will miss his wife. But there's enough love in me to find someone else. Not to replace your father, mind you, but to redirect all this love and maybe, just maybe, carve out my own piece of happy again."

"You sayin' you love me, Elaine?" Sam asked from the doorway.

"I didn't hear you come in," she said softly.

"Doesn't change the fact I did." He looked at Quinn and dipped his chin before looking back at Quinn's mom. "Answer me, Elaine. Please."

"I…" She glanced at Quinn.

"Claim your happy, Mom."

She smiled a watery smile. "Only if you claim yours." Then she did something she hadn't done in a very, very long time. She held out her hand, pinky finger extended. "Pinky swear?"

He hooked his finger with hers and watched as she lifted their linked fingers to her mouth and kissed them.

"Pinky swear," he promised.

Sam stepped forward and his mom moved into the man's embrace.

"I can't believe I'm saying this, but you two should get a room."

She grinned over her shoulder. "Only after you do."

Then they were gone, leaning into each other and sharing whispers and laughter and a short, passionate kiss.

Quinn picked up the button to call his nurse. He would need his discharge papers sooner rather than later. He'd made a promise to his mother that he'd be chasing down his happiness, and he would.

No man of any worth broke a pinky swear made with his mom.

TAYLOR SAT AT her desk at the Jenny Lake ranger's station in Grand Teton National Park and stared out the window. She'd been here for almost a month, working remote areas via ATV, four-wheel-drive vehicles or by hiking in on foot. She had yet to get on a horse, go up in a chopper or come down a rope. She'd been brutally honest in her interview that, while she was trained in those rescue modalities, she wasn't prepared to make them a part of her daily life yet. Someday, she hoped, but not yet. It hadn't hurt that her new therapist had provided all of the documentation needed to validate a workplace accommodation and a letter supporting Taylor's potential for return to a full-duty search-and-rescue schedule within the year. Thanks to the psychologist, Dr. DeLay, Taylor had a plan of attack, one she was executing with precision and persistence as she learned to leave her past behind her.

She'd learned to take those first steps as she approached her recertification.

With Quinn.

Even thinking his name made her heart ache. She would never regret what she'd learned, never regret that she'd found the courage over the course of her time there to lay down the guilt that had almost consumed her and to manage the small bursts that persisted by engaging in activities or reaching out and asking for help. No more excuses. No more hiding. No more retreating to the dark corners of her mind. That was all done.

And at some point, she'd promised herself she would consider the option of opening herself up to love again.

First, though, she had to love herself enough to allow herself to heal. She was a work in progress and damn proud of how far she'd come.

Thinking about specifics brought up some of the more recent events that, while technically in her past, were part of her every waking thought. There were a few mental snapshots she'd recovered in relation to the Rainier event. But there were also things she'd experienced on her last climb.

With Quinn.

He'd treated her with such love, pulling her out of the past with action after action that conveyed how he felt about her, actions that validated everything he'd come to mean to her and her own feelings for the cowboy under the hat.

I love you.

But he'd never said the three words she most needed to hear.

Fissures in her heart that had started to heal cracked all over again. Some of the wounds were shallow, but others were deep enough and hurt enough that she struggled not to clutch her chest. It wasn't like she could force herself to heal. Time would do its job, or it wouldn't.

The IM icon on her computer beeped, and she swiveled her desk chair to face the screen. A few taps of the keys and she was logged in. The avatar of her boss, Aaron Rubio, came up followed by a message.

AR: You set to post updated fire info for backcountry visitors?

TW: Yep. Gear's packed. Plan to head out tomorrow.

AR: Busy now?

Taylor leaned back in her chair and looked into Aaron's office. Why was he messaging her instead of chatting face-to-face? She started to get up and go into his office, but her IM alert sounded again.

AR: I've got the station covered. If you head out now, you can hit Remote Station 18 today. You should go. Now's good.

TW: Okay. Aaron, I ask because I care. Have you been drinking?

AR: LOL

TW: My friend, you're one short step from an intervention.

AR: Sometimes you just need to have a little faith. See you Monday.

Taylor flinched at the "have a little faith" comment. In her experience, asking for even a little faith wasn't enough. All her life, she'd struggled to believe in herself. Counseling explained why—lack of confidence displayed by one or both parents, fear of failure, fear of letting others down, lack of self-confidence at later stages of life, trauma and more. What counseling hadn't done, at least initially, was help her fix the problem. But she'd found a good therapist when she'd moved to Wyoming, and she felt like she was finally on the right path. She'd even managed to have a flashback to the helo crash at Rainier and she'd stayed conscious and functioning through it all.

Her IM sounded again.

AR: Go, Taylor. It'll help me immensely to have you here Monday.

It was the second time he'd mentioned Monday. Seeing as it was only Wednesday, if she left now, she'd still make it back by Saturday. Which gave her plenty of time for error or unanticipated slowdowns. She started to reply with that information when his avatar lit up.

AR: You're still here. Station 18 before dark, Taylor. Today. I've got a hiker registered to go in and I want those new guidelines posted. Guy seems pretty determined to set up camp.

TW: Any reason I should be concerned he's setting up camp in a dry zone?

AR: Only if the updated fire restrictions aren't posted before sundown. Have your ass out of that chair in 60 seconds and through the door in 90. Clock starts now.

She laughed and signed off, grabbed her pack and was out the door with at least five seconds to spare.

THE BACKCOUNTRY IN Wyoming was so different than in Washington. Both had one thing in common, though. They were inherently beautiful. Grand Teton was just its own creature. There was a remoteness to it that resonated with her, soothing the ache in her when life got too heavy. She'd escaped here more than once over the last five years. Coming here instead of returning to Washington had seemed like a prudent move.

The trail to Station 18 was relatively easy to follow. Every now and then she'd come across signs of human passage or animal interest, but nothing major. With summer approaching and park attendance anticipated to be higher this year than ever before, it made sense to watch for any conflict between guests and permanent residents.

Scrambling down a small hillside instead of taking the switchback trail, Taylor paused at the stream running through the bottom of the little canyon. The air was so clean here, the silence absolute. Except for the sound of footsteps approaching.

She stood and moved off the trail, retrieving her government-issued sidearm. It was foolish to fear the sound of every breaking twig or footfall on a mapped path, but when she was the only person registered to be out this far? It paid to be cautious.

Watching the path, gun at her side, she saw the man crest the hill, look around and start down the same way she had—scramble versus switchback. Something about him tripped her memory and her heart rate began to climb.

Broad shoulders.

Narrow hips.

Long legs.

Dark hair that flipped around a worn shirt collar.

Cowboy hat.

Right arm in a sling.

She had no doubt the dark eyes would be framed with enviable lashes or that a genuine smile would sink a dimple to the left of full lips.

Quinn Monroe.

Heart in her throat, she stepped onto the trail.

He let out a small *eep* of surprise and then blushed.

Did he have to be so charming? Or delicious? Or panty-melting hot?

"Do you always pull a gun on your lover?" he asked and, yep, there was that dimple.

Taylor holstered her gun and forced herself to smile in return. "Nope."

"I'm the exception, then."

"No, Quinn." She braced herself. "I'm not your lover."

Something so much stronger than hurt—anguish?—flashed in his eyes. Jaw working, he shrugged his good shoulder. "How are you, Taylor?"

"How am I...?" She shook her head, trying to clear it of the questions pinging around all willy-nilly. "I'm good. Fine."

He took a step toward her. "Which is it, Taylor? Good or fine?"

She retreated a step. "They're the same thing." He wouldn't hurt her. No way. But he had the power, using only words, to shatter her heart. Keeping her distance would be prudent.

"No, baby. They aren't."

Baby.

Her heart lurched toward him, the reprobate.

He kept coming, slowly but surely, his eyes always on hers. "It's not the same, Taylor. It's like if you asked me if I was living or alive."

"Again, the same."

"They aren't, though." He paused and stuck his good hand in the front pocket of his jeans. "I'm certainly alive. My heart's beating, I'm breathing, I've got serious butterflies in my stomach." He rested his hand there, as if to still them.

"Butterflies?" she murmured.

He nodded. "Bad. But while those are proof I'm alive, they don't prove I'm living. 'Alive' implies my involuntary systems are doing their thing. If they quit, I'd be on life support not living support, right?"

Seriously? First her boss and his weird behavior, and now Quinn and his alive/living comparison.

"*Living* implies active involvement. It means I'm engaged in the world around me, I'm experiencing the joys and the heartaches, the highs and lows, acknowledging the benign moments that pass but committing to memory the moments with immeasurable value. See the difference?"

Her boss kicking her out of the office... Quinn being on the trail...their paths crossing... Son of a bitch.

"How do you know my boss?"

"Aaron?" Quinn looked at his feet, for all the world like a little boy and not the heartbreaker he was. "Went to college with him."

"You set this up," she all but snarled. "What, Quinn? So afraid of what I'd say that you had to trick me to meet you here?" More fissures in her heart, these deeper and far more consequential, broke open. "Could you not have just asked to speak to me?"

He looked up at that, and she took an involuntary step backward at the fire burning in his gaze. Her pack scraped a tree and she stepped aside, shedding the massive weight.

"And if I'd asked you, Taylor? What then? Can you honestly tell me you would have been happy to meet for a cup of coffee? I need to…" He rolled his shoulder then pulled his hat off, gripping it hard enough to roll the brim. "I need to apologize to you."

"Apology accepted," she replied, voice shaking. Her heart was breaking with him here, seeing his still-recovering shoulder and arm, hearing the timbre of his voice and recognizing small tells in his movements. She had to go, had to get out of here. French cooking school was sounding better and better.

What he said next stopped her in her tracks. "You were absolutely right. On the mountain, I mean. About all of it."

With precise steps and infinite care, lest she tangle her feet up and land in the creek, she faced him. "I appreciate that, but…" She blew out a harsh breath. "Quinn, I don't know what you want, but—"

"You," he blurted out. "A chance with you. Every bit of you. The good and the bad, the strong and the weak, the hope and the heartache, the sunrises and sunsets, the successes and the failures—mine and yours." He tossed his hat aside and strode toward her, stopping within a few feet. "I want you to be the first person I see in the morning and the last person I see at night. I want to hear your voice in the barn and the kitchen and the shower and the bedroom." He lifted his good hand, reaching for her, but then withdrew and let it rest at his side. "I want to tell you I love you a dozen times a day. I want to say it until you're so steeped in the truth of it that there's no room for doubt."

"You hurt me, Quinn." She thumped her fist over her heart, surprised there wasn't an echo. "You *hurt* me. How can you expect me to believe you've miraculously developed unconditional faith in me? Faith you didn't have on the mountain when I needed it—needed *you*—most? I left you then because I knew I needed to stand on my own two feet, to come back to the job, and life, I'd worked so hard to create. You showed me that walking away wasn't the answer, and I'll forever be grateful for that. But you were also perfectly clear that what there was between us wasn't supposed to be long term. If it had been, you would've…" She snapped her jaw shut. If he turned her away, a part of her she'd only just coaxed back to life would be gone.

Forever irretrievable. Instead, she focused on the tangible argument. "What's changed? Why come all this way just to make sure I know you have faith in me? Because I'm standing here aching with the need to believe you, but I've got nothing to go on."

"You want me to have faith in you, right?" She nodded, and he held out a hand. "I want you to have faith in me. Meet me halfway, Taylor."

She wanted to. Man, she wanted to. Her feet tingled and her thighs twitched with the need to step forward. What happened next finished her.

He took a step forward. Just one. Paused. Then he took another. Paused again. He kept it up until his outstretched hand was inches away from her.

"I believe in you entirely, Taylor. So if you won't come to me, if I haven't earned that trust, I'll come to you. A hundred steps, a thousand steps or a million steps, it doesn't matter. I will keep coming to you because I have faith in you and in us. This is it for me. *You're* it. I will cross the distance over and over until you're ready, Taylor. Until you look at me and realize that I will spend every day of the rest of my life, of *our* lives, showing you just how much I believe in you."

He said everything she'd always wanted to hear, laid waste to her reservations and left her speechless in the process. And that proved to be a problem. When she didn't respond, he nodded once.

"I respect the fact that you may need some time. I also respect the fact that just because I feel this way doesn't mean you do, too."

"No!" she blurted, lunging after him as he stepped away.

He froze. "No, what?"

"I…" Her hands were shaking and sweaty. How could

she be all sweaty *now*? She looked up and, before she could come up with the thousand and one reasons this was insane, she held out her hand. He reached for it and she yanked it back, scrubbing her palm on her uniform pants. "Sorry," she whispered…and held it out again.

Quinn reached for her, more slowly this time, pausing with less than a hair's breadth between their palms. "Taylor?"

She tore her gaze away from their almost-there-just-another-smidge-and-they'd-touch hands, and met his open stare, following it down as he went to one knee.

"A wise woman explained to me why the words *I love you* should never be used to say goodbye. They're strong words, words with the power to change time and places and people." He reached into his shirt pocket and pulled out a little packet of tissue paper, considering it as he spoke. "They're words that are too big for a moment but, instead, require a lifetime to explore. They should have shared memories and inside jokes and private moments pinned all over them. I want to give you that, Taylor. I want a do-over, but life's finicky that way. So I'll do this instead and hope I get it right." He drew in a deep breath, puffed out his cheeks and blew the air out hard and fast. Then he looked up at her and, taking her hand, put the little packet in her palm and curled her fingers over it. He held her hand that way, seeming to struggle to find the next step.

She had that covered. "I love you, Quinn Monroe."

He was off the ground in a flash, hauling her against him with his good arm and whispering unintelligible words into her hair. Several seconds passed before they stopped shaking so hard she wasn't sure who held up whom.

"I missed you so much," she said into his chest.

"Look at me."

As if the last month hadn't happened, as if he was still

her instructor, she lifted her chin. Their eyes met. And he sealed the deal. "I love you, Taylor Williams." He tipped his head toward the paper. "Will you open that for me?"

Fingers trembling, she unfolded the blue tissue paper to reveal an eternity band with asscher-cut stones that alternated between deep emerald green and colorless white fire.

"I don't see you in something that's going to snag or get in your way. You're not that woman. You're steady and present and wholly there. There's no break in the stones on the ring, honey, because that way there is no beginning and no end. There just is. That's what I want for us, now and always."

She shifted the ring back and forth, watching through tears as the light burned in each stone.

He rose to stand before her and spoke with passionate humility that tore down any final reservations she might have harbored. "Today. Tomorrow. A thousand tomorrows. I will never have enough time to tell you I love you, but I will always fight for just one more day." He reached out and tucked a lock of her hair behind one ear. "And I have absolute faith that if, and when, I screw up, you're the only woman with the skill set to fix my blunder. Do me the honor of loving me in return. Marry me, Taylor, and let me spend every day of my life showing you what forever means."

"Yes," she breathed. "On one condition."

"Name it."

"Take me home." She slipped the ring onto her finger and curled her fingers over it as he moved into her, lowering his lips to hers and kissing her with tender ferocity.

He lifted his head and met her stare head on. "Ranching isn't an easy life."

"I never asked for easy."

He grinned. "And look what it got you."

She reached up and pulled him toward her, whispering her answer against his lips. "It got me everything I never knew I wanted."

* * * * *

If you loved this novel, don't miss
Kelli Ireland's WILD WESTERN HEAT *miniseries,*
available now from Harlequin Blaze!

A COWBOY RETURNS
COWBOY PROUD
COWBOY STRONG

Get 2 Free Books,
Plus 2 Free Gifts—
just for trying the Reader Service!

◆HARLEQUIN *Desire*

SPECIAL EXCERPT FROM

HARLEQUIN

Blaze

There's no way Lola Whittaker is going to rekindle the flames between her and sexy smoke jumper Erik McKnight—she still hasn't forgiven him for the past.

Read on for a sneak preview of
UP IN FLAMES,
the newest Kira Sinclair title from Harlequin Blaze!

"Lola. It's good to see you."

"Erik. I can't say the same."

That wasn't strictly true. Because even as anger—anger she'd been harboring for the last six years—burst through her, she couldn't stop her gaze from rippling down his body.

He was bigger—pure muscle. Considering the work he did now, that was no surprise. Smoke jumping wasn't for weaklings. It was, however, for daredevils and adrenaline junkies. Erik McKnight was both.

Hurt flashed through his eyes. "I'm sorry you still feel that way."

Wow, so he'd finally issued her an apology. Hardly for the right reasons, though.

"What are you doing here?"

"Didn't your dad or Colt tell you?"

Her anger now had a new direction. The men in her life were all oblivious morons.

"I'm—" his gaze pulled away, focusing on the sky behind her "—taking a couple months off."

Six years ago she would have asked for an explanation. Today she didn't want to care, so she kept her mouth shut.

"Came home to spend some time with Mom. Your dad's letting me pick up some shifts at the station."

Lola nodded. "Well, good luck with that." Hooking her thumb over her shoulder, she said, "I'm just gonna go…"

"Do anything that gets you far away from me."

She shrugged. He wasn't wrong, but her mother had raised her to be too polite to say so.

"You look good, Lola. I…I really am glad we ran into each other."

Was he serious? Lola stared at him for several seconds, searching his face before she realized that he was. Which made the anger bubbling up inside her finally burst free.

"Did you take a hit to the head, Erik? You act like I haven't been right here for the past six years, exactly where you left me when you ran away. Ran away when my brother was lying in a hospital bed, broken and bleeding."

"Because I put him there." Erik's gruff voice whispered over her.

"You're right. You did."

"That right there is why I left. I could see it every time you looked at me."

"See what?"

"Blame." His stark expression ripped through her. A small part of her wanted to reach out to him and offer comfort.

But he was right. She did blame him. For so many things.

Don't miss
UP IN FLAMES by Kira Sinclair,
available May 2017 wherever
Harlequin® Blaze® books and ebooks are sold.

www.Harlequin.com

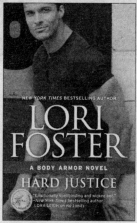

Turn your love of reading into rewards you'll love with

Harlequin My Rewards

Join for FREE today at www.HarlequinMyRewards.com

Earn **FREE BOOKS** of your choice.

Experience **EXCLUSIVE OFFERS** and contests.

Enjoy **BOOK RECOMMENDATIONS** selected just for you.

PLUS! Sign up now and get **500** points right away!

Earn **FREE** REWARDS
HarlequinMyRewards.com
Join Today!

MYR16R

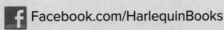